When the Mountain Sings

When the Mountain Sings

JOHN MACLEAN

HOUGHTON MIFFLIN COMPANY • BOSTON 1992

Library of Congress Cataloging-in-Publication Data

MacLean, John, 1945-
   When the mountain sings / John MacLean.
      p. cm.
   Summary: Thirteen-year-old competitive skier Sam experiences
the excitement and intensity of preparing for his first championship
race.
   ISBN 0-395-59917-2
   [1. Skis and skiing — Fiction.]   I. Title.
PZ7.M22434Wh   1992   91-26720
[Fic] — dc20   CIP
                             AC

HAD 10 9 8 7 6 5 4 3 2 1

This is a work of fiction and all the
characters are fictional.

For
Gillean, Simon, Alexander, Morgan
with love

*The mountains and the hills before you
shall break forth into singing
and all the trees of the field shall
clap their hands.*

One

IT'S SATURDAY MORNING and the sun is never going to rise. It's so cold the air is heavier than ice. It's too cold to talk, so we just stand there with our necks pulled into our collars. I make fists with my hands inside the palms of my gloves. The empty fingers flap like frozen pennants. We stamp our ski boots to keep warm.

We're in a grove of eighty-foot pine trees next to the race shack; waiting for Phil, waiting for the January sun to rise. I know Phil is coming, but I don't think the sun is. It probably got frozen to the horizon, like the pine needles that are frozen in the snow underneath our boots. If it does rise it'll sneak up behind the mountain and suddenly be there. Phil won't sneak up on us. He'll come over the horizon like a winter storm.

There are seven of us who race with Phil: five guys and two girls, but no one could tell that from looking at us wrapped up in our down parkas and warm-up pants, ski hats pulled low over our foreheads, goggles over our eyes, and scarves around our faces. It's ten above zero.

We're the only ones dumb enough to be out here. The

older racers and younger racers don't start until nine. They're all inside the lodge sitting by the fire or playing videos while we're out here freezing to death. Phil likes us to be early. He likes us to push ourselves beyond our comfort zone, whatever that means.

"Where is he?" someone moans.

The scarf around my mouth is frozen with ice crystals from my breath, so I don't say anything. I just stand there lifting one boot, then the other, curling and uncurling my toes, wondering why I ever got into alpine racing.

"Let's go." A voice flashes across the frozen snow. We turn and Phil is whirling toward us. The hood of his red parka is pulled over his head and tied tight around his face. His goggles are strapped around his hood and pressed over his eyes. He swings his arms and stomps the heels of his ski boots into the hard-packed snow. He looks like someone who's already climbed Mount Everest and is ready for K2.

"Well, what are you waiting for?" He claps his ski gloves together. "Let's go, let's go, time's a wasting. We got a race tomorrow. Let's get the poles out of the race shack."

The race shack has been here since I started skiing ten years ago. It's a rickety building that the coaches built on a weekend with warped two-by-fours and sheets of cheap plywood grooved to look like siding. It's stained brown and there's a row of windows on the second floor that looks up the mountain. That's where the officials stay warm when they're timing races. On the first floor there are coaches' lockers, a wax room, and a storage area in the back for racing gear. Phil opens the door where the bamboo poles are stored and pulls out bundles of red and blue poles. We throw the bundles over our shoulders. He grabs a leather belt and holster and buckles it around his waist. He takes a blue Makita drill with a foot-long stainless steel bit and sticks it in the holster.

"Sam, go inside and grab me a battery pack off the workbench."

I lean my bundle of poles against a pine tree and kick open the side door. Inside the shack it's warm. The walls are lined with pink insulation and wooden lockers. I go into the wax room. The long workbench is littered with screwdrivers, files, broken bindings, waxing irons, candy wrappers, empty Styrofoam coffee cups, old ski gloves with torn fingers, old rolls of duct tape. I find the charger underneath a half-empty bag of bread that's gone moldy blue. I grab the thin, black battery pack and go back outside. Phil puts the pack in his pocket. I throw the bundle of poles onto my shoulders.

"You guys ready?" Phil slams the door shut.

No one answers.

"Geez, you guys are a bunch of stiffs. What's the matter? You cold?"

Yeah. We nod. The fact is, we're freezing to death.

"Well, let's get going. We'll warm up when we skate over to Mountain Meadow." Mountain Meadow is an intermediate slope as wide as a runway; it's good for cruising through the big, fast turns of Giant Slalom.

Phil throws his skis on the snow and steps into the bindings, puts a bundle of bamboo poles over his shoulder, and starts off. We step into our bindings and skate after him in single file. With the red and blue poles over our shoulders we ski down a little slope, past the pond where water is stored for the snow guns. We skate up the side of the beginner's slope, down around the J-bar tower, and over to the green chair lift. The loading platform for the chair lift is fifty yards up the slope. With those poles on our shoulders, we have to skate low and hard to make it. When we get in line most of us are panting, our breaths like snow shot out of snow guns. I ride up the lift with Felix, the poles resting across our knees. Even though we're good friends it's too cold to talk, so we disappear inside our parkas as far as we can.

We get off the chair at the top of Mountain Meadow and snowplow a couple of hundred yards across the flats to where the crest of the hill begins. Phil takes out the Makita and drills two holes in the snow twenty inches apart. The electric engine whirs and clicks in the freezing cold as snow spirals up the bit. When he pulls out the drill there's a hole in the slope the size of a whale's blowhole. I can almost see a thread of steam spiraling out of each hole. It makes me think that maybe the mountain is alive. Phil jabs a bamboo pole into each hole and tells us this will be our starting gate. Then he snowplows down the hill about twenty yards, skates off to the side, drills a third hole, and jabs in a blue pole. This will be our first gate. He continues down the mountain, stopping every twenty to thirty yards to put in either a blue or a red gate. Before he drills he looks up the hill to make certain that the gates are offset enough so that we will have to carve strong and powerful turns to make our way through the course. We snowplow after him, clearing away the loose snow from the gates so the course will be smooth when we start our practice runs.

By the time we get to the bottom, the sun has risen, spreading itself across the mountain, and the frigid air has begun to slink off into the woods. It's warming up enough so that skiing won't be an exercise in frostbite, and might actually be fun. As we start to skate over to the chair lift, Phil calls me. I stop. He skis up to me, his parka sleeve curled over the extra blue and red bamboo poles on his shoulder.

"You've been skiing okay, Sam."

"Thanks," I mumble, wondering what's coming next. I've been skiing with Phil for over a year now and I never know what he's going to do or say.

"You're beginning to carve your turns and you're working hard. I think it's time you started racing."

"You mean racing in races racing?"

"Yeah, I want you to come with us tomorrow. We're going to leave at six. Sam, are you listening to me?"

"I don't know if I'm ready, Phil." Practicing racing and racing in races are two different things. Practicing racing is fun. Racing in races is not fun. It's like the difference between being killed in a play and being killed in real life. Being killed in a play is fun. Being killed in real life is murder.

"Sure you're ready. I wouldn't tell you that you were ready if you weren't. We're leaving here at six, so be at the parking lot a little before."

"Six? That means I've got to get up at five."

"More like quarter of."

"Quarter of?" Racing's murder.

* ——————— **TWO** ——————— *

"SAM."

A voice as far away as snow falling in the pines settles over me.

"Sam, wake up."

My shoulders start shaking and the bed starts to rumble underneath me.

"Wake up."

"Huh?" I try to open an eye. It's Bo. A light in the hall shines over his shoulder so that his face is in shadow.

"Time to get up."

"What . . . time . . . is it?"

"Quarter of."

"Quarter of what?"

"Five."

"Five?" I pull a pillow over my head. Forget it. Quarter of five's no time for a normal thirteen-year-old to be getting up.

"Come on. Or you'll miss the race."

Race? I'm not racing. I'm staying here in bed where it's soft and comfortable and . . .

"Sam."

Under the pillow I hear Bo flick on the overhead light.

And I can feel the cold air that's been hiding in the dark corners of the room come flashing over me.

"Time to rise and shine."

Right.

"Time to shower and shave."

I don't shave.

"Time to whoosh down the mountainside."

Time to whoosh up your mouth.

"You have five minutes to shower. Ten minutes to breakfast."

"Right."

"Ten minutes."

"I said, right."

"Not so loud. The cat's sleeping. The dog's sleeping. The fish are sleeping."

"Well, you just get out of here." We don't even have a dog.

* —————— Three —————— *

I STAND OVER the cold bathtub, feeling the water with the back of my hand. It's so cold in the bathroom that the faucet starts steaming even before the water turns hot. When it finally gets warm I climb into the tub, pull the curtain shut, adjust the water, and flick on the shower. I lean back into the hot spray, my hands gauging the heat of the water. Slowly I open my eyes. The shower curtain is clear plastic, with a map of the world printed over it. The oceans are blue. The lands are mostly green and orange, yellow and pink, the colors of ski parkas. My eyes always seem to rest on Greenland, Alaska, Finland. I wonder what it's like to be in a place where the sun never rises or never sets. I step closer to the shower so the water pours over my head.

How did I get into this racing? I never started out to race. It just sort of happened. I was three when Mom got the idea that Bo and I should have skiing lessons. Bo was six. Our teacher had freckles and long, blond hair that hung in a braid down her back. Her name was Mary. First Mary taught us to put on our skis. Then she taught us to walk with our skis. We were in front of the main lodge heading toward the race shack. Bo kept racing ahead, yelling encouragement at me.

I stared down at my feet. They were stuffed into stiff leather boots with bright steel buckles that were cranked so tight I couldn't feel them. And the boots were strapped to the skis with a cable that was bound so tightly around my heels I knew that if I tried to move an inch I'd fall flat on my face.

"Slide those skis." Mary smiled at me.

Bo almost pranced on his. If he had gotten close enough I would have whacked him with one of my ski poles, except I was having a hard time holding on to them with my frozen mittens.

I tried to slide my skis and fell face first. There I was, my face pressed into the snow, my goggles squashed against my chin, my arms and legs and skis sprawled out like a dead starfish. Mary somehow untangled me, rolled me onto my back, pulled the goggles off my chin, and wiped the freezing snow off my face with her scarf.

"Sam," I remember her singing. "Sam, Sam."

Sam, Sam, I sang to myself.

She finally got me to stand, straightened my hat, adjusted my scarf, and promised me hot cocoa if I made it to the race shack and back. I looked at Bo, his blond curls spilling out of his yellow hat, his cheeks apple red. He had already been to the race shack and back about fifteen thousand times. Mary put my poles between the palm and thumb of my mittens and gently bent the frozen material around the shaft. I fell a couple of hundred more times before she gave up and decided to pull me. She was red in the face, her parka was unzipped, her hat and skis were off. After she got me to stand, she took the ends of my poles and began to pull.

"Don't fall," she almost cried. "Please, don't fall."

I tried as hard as she was trying to smile not to fall, and sometime in the late morning we finally made it to the race shack. It felt as if it took us most of the winter. Bo looked as if he had grown. Mary looked as if she had aged.

"Good job, Sam." She reached down and gave me a hug. When she let go I fell.

"Sam." There's a knock on the bathroom door. "What are you doing in there?"

"Thinking."

"Yeah? Well, it's time for breakfast."

Yeah. I turn off the shower. I wonder what happened to Mary. We had her for one or two more lessons, then she kind of disappeared.

— 9 —

Four

I PULL A TOWEL off the rack and wrap it around my waist. The room is filled with mist. I step out onto the tiles. The last thing I want to do is leave this warm bathroom and go freeze on some stupid mountain. I run back to my room. It's even colder in there. I grab my long johns and jump under the covers. I'm a little wet and the sheets have cooled off, but it's warmer than the room. I pull on my long underwear pants, struggle with the shirt. Then I throw off the covers and run downstairs on tiptoes. The hall is dark and cold. The stairs squeak. In the living room the wood-burning stove is cranking. I stand by it. A kettle on top of the stove is rattling, steam bubbling out from underneath the top and misting the air. I can feel the heat of the stove through my long johns. I can hear Mom in the kitchen.

I sit down at the piano and start playing a Simon and Garfunkel song I had to memorize for my sixties-type piano teacher. She's pure granola, but she's not a bad teacher, and it's not a bad song. The chords are soft and gentle, and I have to stretch my fingers to reach all the notes, since my hands are those of a kid who is only 5 feet 3 inches. The right-hand melody reminds me of water running over stones. The left hand bridges the chords.

"Nice," Mom calls from the kitchen.

"Thanks." I stop playing and look at her. She's standing in front of the stove wearing a bathrobe and felt-lined boots. Her red hair is pulled back in a ponytail. I get up from the piano and turn on the light to the aquarium. I open the top and the smell of warm water bubbles up at me. I take a pinch of fish food and sprinkle it across the surface. The guppies flash to the top and peck at it. The angels glide toward the surface. The only things moving are the tiny fins twirling at their sides. The neons dart at the flakes as they sink. Blue and orange, they are like bits of stained glass.

"Mom?" I study the backs of the neons.

"Yeah?"

"Where are the neons from?"

"The pet store."

I close the top and walk into the kitchen. She's dragging a spatula backward through a yellow puddle of eggs.

"Why don't you butter those English muffins?" she asks.

I open the glass door and pull the muffins out of the toaster oven. "Seriously, Mom, where are they from?"

"If they're English, chances are from England."

"I'm talking about the fish," I almost shout.

"I don't know." She lifts the frying pan off the burner, scrapes the eggs onto a couple of plates, and hands one to me. "Bo, breakfast," she calls.

We sit down at the table. I watch the steam curling off the eggs, then look up and watch Bo walk into the room. He's already got his blue sweats on and a white turtleneck. I'm still in my long underwear. I can't get over how big Bo is. He seems to grow every night. He's gone from being big for his age to being six foot three, and with his red curls he looks even taller. If he were my age and I were his age we'd probably be the same height. But Bo's not my age. He's sixteen and races with the older kids, called I's and II's. I race with kids who are thirteen to fifteen. We're called III's. I don't know why.

"Nice to see you finally got up." Bo sits down next to me, grabs one of my muffins, rips it in half, and takes the largest piece.

"Hey."

"It was burned," he says with his mouth full.

"Want some breakfast, Bo?" Mom hands Bo a plate.

"Sure." He takes the plate.

"Where are you racing today?" she asks.

"Wachusetts," Bo answers between forkfuls.

"What about you, Sam?"

"I forget," I answer.

"Bousquet," Bo answers for me. "It's a good mountain."

Mom looks at my plate. "Aren't you going to eat?" Then she looks at Bo. "I think Sam's nervous."

"I'm not nervous." I push the eggs toward the back of the plate. "I just don't want to race. I mean eat."

"I'm nervous and this is my third year of racing." Bo finishes his eggs. "You're always going to be nervous."

"I'm not nervous. I just don't want to race. I'm not ready to race."

"That's not what Phil says." Bo drinks from his glass of milk.

"What does Phil say?" Mom asks.

"He says Sam's been skiing well enough to race since last year. I've seen him skiing with Phil and the guys. I mean, geez" — he holds his palms up in the air — "I ski with him every day myself. He skis as well as any kid his age."

"Right."

"That is right." He finishes his milk. "The only part about skiing you have to figure out, Sam, is how to ski as well in a race as you do in practice."

"Yeah, well, in practice you have the whole day and no tension. But in a race all you have is two runs and lots of tension."

"That's exactly what I'm saying. It takes a while to learn how not to let your nerves get in your way."

"Yeah? Well, I haven't learned yet."

"And the only way you're going to learn is to race."

"Great," I mumble.

Mom nods her head. "That sounds reasonable. If Phil thinks you're ready, you probably are." She reaches across the table. "What's this?" she asks pulling a hair out of my chin. "I thought you said you weren't shaving."

"Ow." I pull away from her hand. "With you around I'll never have to shave."

"I think Mom's nervous." Bo picks up his plate and goes to the sink.

"I think Mom's weird."

"Well, I am nervous and I'm not even racing. Now that is weird."

"Weird or not we got to go in five minutes," Bo says as he walks toward the mud room. "I'll start the car."

"And I'll get dressed." Mom puts her cup in the sink.

I eat half of my eggs, put the plate in the sink, and

go put the liners back in my ski boots. My feet sweat so much when I ski that if I don't take the liners out to dry, the next day I ski the liners freeze into blocks of ice. And my feet inside the liners freeze and hurt so bad, especially when they begin to thaw. Drying out my liners is something I've learned to do the hard way. Just about how I've learned everything. I put the boots in my red duffel bag. They're a lot different from the ones I used when I was little. These are racing boots. Bright yellow with black buckles. I pull on my gray sweat pants and my white turtleneck. I put my goggles, gloves, and mitts in the duffel and pull on my blue parka. I throw the duffel over my shoulder. In the kitchen I toss a couple of sandwiches and a box of juice in the bag. In the mud room I grab my K2s; they're black TN comps with blue lettering fading into purple — and they cruise. I grab my poles and hike out to the car. Except for the headlights on the snow it's as black as outer space. The air is so cold it takes my breath away. My boots squeak in the snow. The sky is crazy with stars. And it's crazy to be only thirteen and leaving home at five-forty in the morning to race down some freezing, cold mountain.

✳———— Five ————✳

THERE ARE THREE cars idling in the dark of the parking lot. Ours and two others. No Phil. We just sit there with the pickup gently rocking back and forth on its springs, the heater blowing hot air at our feet, the radio playing music that sounds like starlight. Mom's channel. Bo and Mom are talking. What they're saying isn't boring. I hear the words, but something's filtering the meaning out of them. Mostly I'm wishing I were someplace else. I don't want to race. I don't want to come in dead last. I know I'm going to come in dead last. I'm just going to embarrass myself and embarrass Phil. He's got so many good racers, he doesn't need me.

He's got Felix and Duncan, two of the best fifteen-year-olds in the state. Duncan is steady and strong and he skis steady and strong. Felix is smaller than Duncan. He's less steady but more acrobatic. He has to be, because he's always getting himself out of a jam. That's just the kind of kid he is. I've known him since I was three and he's always taken chances as if he thinks he's charmed. I don't know how he got to be that way. His mother's a bookkeeper and his father runs heavy equipment, and they never buy lottery tickets. Duncan's parents are from Japan and hardly speak English. His father's some kind of scientist at the university, but that doesn't keep him from coming to all of Duncan's practices. He walks up the mountain and you can tell he's looking for Duncan's brown parka and black pants by the way his face lights up when Duncan and the rest of us ski past.

Then there's Josh and Louie; they've been racing for two years. Josh is fourteen; he's small and reminds me of a little furry animal. I don't know why. Maybe it's his small mouth and thick eyebrows. He skis a lot like Felix but without taking the chances. His parents are born-again Christians and there's not much room for error in his life. Louie's just the opposite. His parents are divorced. His mother is always taking chances with different guys and his father is always taking chances in different bars. Louie's life is like a VCR on fast forward. He's my age but he's the biggest kid on the team. He's got broad shoulders, as if he's lifted weights or taken steroids, and he's already shaving.

A horn blares across the parking lot. Mom and Bo stop talking and look up. Coming straight at us is a set of headlights on high beam. As they get closer I can make out the grille of a Dodge van. Everything I know about Phil prepares me for what's going to happen next, so I only half close my eyes. Two hundred feet away he steps on his brakes, spins his front wheels, and skids the van around 180 degrees. It rocks to a stop a hundred feet from us. Phil jumps out, takes off his K2 baseball cap, and holds it in the air as if he just hit a home run. All I can think of is, it's a good thing Phil doesn't drink.

"Race time!" He waves his hat in the air. "Let's go, dudes."

"Geez." Bo looks at me shaking his head. "I sometimes forget what it's like to race with Phil."

"Hubba, hubba." Phil puts his hat back on his head.

Duncan, Felix, and Molly are already in the van. Louie gets out of one car. Josh and Leah climb out of another. I can tell by the way their shoulders are slumped that they'd rather be sleeping.

"Phil doesn't usually drive like that, does he, Bo?" Mom has question-mark wrinkles around her eyes.

"Well, Ma, being with Phil is like being on a mission."

"What is that supposed to mean?"

"It's like being on a planetary probe or something."

A black Jeep Wagoneer pulls up next to us, its engine roaring at a high idle. It's Tom, Bo's coach. He's already picked up Jim, Alex, and Mac, three of Bo's teammates. Bo gets out of the truck and grabs his skis and bag and comes around to Mom's side.

Mom winds down her window. "Bo, Phil's not into crystals or UFOs is he?"

"Just racing, Mom."

"What did you mean by planetary probe?"

"Just that skiing for Phil is like exploring the universe. It's a once-in-a-lifetime experience. That's all." And then to me, "Good luck, Sam."

"Yeah, you too."

I watch him throw his stuff in the back of the Wagoneer. Then I grab my skis and bag out of the back and walk slowly around to Mom's door. The Wagoneer pulls out. Tom beeps his horn and Bo and the guys wave. I wave back.

"Have fun, Sam," Mom says.

The way she says it I don't know if it's a question or a statement, so I just say, "Yeah."

Six

"MORNING, DUDE." Phil takes my skis and poles and slides them into the flat wooden box on top of the van. He grabs my duffel bag and throws it into the back. I open the sliding door. It's like a bunk room inside — the windows are steamed up, the bags are stacked in the back, and there are three rows of bench-seats with a couple of kids in each, except in the back where there's a place next to Felix. I start making my way toward him.

Josh raises his eyebrows. "Morning, Sam." It's so warm in the van he's wearing only his gray ribbed undershirt.

I sidle past him. "Morning."

"Morning, Sam."

I can tell it's Duncan by his voice, but I can't see him. "Morning."

"Morning, Sam." Molly's voice is so soft and high I can barely hear it. I say good morning back and try to squeeze past her and Leah. Leah doesn't say anything. She never says much in the morning. Maybe it's the retainer she has to wear. Maybe she's too tired to talk. They're both wearing turtlenecks. Molly's is new and dark blue, Leah's is old and faded red.

"Leah," I mumble as I pass her. She nods.

"Morning, Felix." He's wearing a Dead T-shirt and blue Descent pants with red stripes down the side, and white plastic shields over the shins, knees, and thighs. He looks like a half-dressed warrior. I sit down next to him, unzip my parka, and as I pull it off, look across the back of the seats. Duncan's sitting up front. Shotgun. That's where the number-one skier sits.

"Morning, dude." Felix slaps me on the leg. "Not a bad spin, huh? I'd say it was over a hundred and eighty degrees. How'd it look from where you were?"

"Not bad."

"From in here it was awesome. You guys must have peed in your pants."

"Mom almost did."

"Felix. Sam." Leah turns and looks at me. It's the first time she's spoken to me this early in the morning. "There's a young girl in here." Leah's not proper. She's anything but proper. She just kind of mothers Molly. Molly's only twelve and the only reason she's racing with our age group is that she's athletic, a fast learner, a fast skier, and Phil's daughter.

"Yeah, Sam, watch your mouth." Felix smiles. His eyes are charged with something that makes them glow. Maybe it's his smile. He's always been like that, even when he's down, which is almost never; his eyes, his whole face, kind of glow. And his teeth are as white and straight as his hair is black and curly. "There are two young ladies among us."

"Can it!" Leah scolds.

"Right." I feel stupid. First for kind of telling on Mom and second for being corrected.

"All right." Phil snaps open the front door, leaps into the driver's seat, and slams the door in a single, simple motion. He pulls on his seat belt. "Have we got a quorum?"

"What?" we all ask together.

"You guys." Phil turns in his seat, takes off his blue K2 hat, rubs his scalp, and cradles the hat back down on his head. Phil's thirty-six but already he has as little hair as my grandfather. That's why he's always wearing baseball hats. He's got a hat for every ski made and for every major league team, but mostly he wears the blue K2 or the pale green Rossignol hat. Like my grandfather, the lack of hair doesn't make him a nerd; in fact, it has just the opposite effect. "You guys, if you don't listen to me you're never going to learn anything. Last Saturday I used the word *quorum* and nobody knew what it meant. So I told you. Wasn't anyone listening?"

We look at each other, hoping one of us knows what Phil's talking about, or at least knows the meaning of the word. Duncan huddles close to the door. Felix sinks into the seat and disappears right next to me. Leah smiles, her lips spread wide over her retainer. Josh burrows his head into his arms. Louie curls his lip. Phil looks straight at me. His eyes — how I imagine lasers to be — burn the length of the van, nearly blinding me. I can feel my eyes beginning to water. I rub them with the back of my hand. I know what's coming next.

"Sam."

That's my name. Please, don't burn holes in my eyes.

"Have we a quorum?"

I close my eyes and guess. "Yes."

"You're correct. We have a quorum. There's a majority of the team here, seven out of seven, so if we wanted to vote we could. But we're not voting. I was using the word loosely to imply that everyone that's going with me is here. Do you follow me?"

We nod.

"If you guys can think at six o'clock in the morning in the parking lot of Thunder Mountain, you're going to be able to think on the mountain. But guys, you have to think. If you don't think, you don't win races. You understand, Sam?"

I nod.

He turns around, puts the van in drive, and we start out the parking lot. "Are we settled?"

"Yeah," a few of us mumble.

"If you're not settled, get settled. We have an hour and fifteen minutes to Bousquet. So unzip your parkas. Loosen your boots. Get comfortable. Fasten your seat belts. My name is Phil and I am your coach. Our air speed will be approximately sixty miles per hour. That's fifty miles an hour into a head wind of ten miles an hour."

"That makes air speed only forty," Felix contradicts him.

"Ah. A voice in the wilderness. At least we know Felix is alive and that a certain amount of information is registering. Very good. I'm pleased. Aren't you pleased, Duncan?"

"Yeah, I'm pleased." Duncan smiles.

"We are all pleased. Are we not all pleased?" Phil is almost singing.

"Yes!" we shout.

"Yes what?"

"Yes, we are all pleased."

"Good. We shall be cruising south on 8A. We will go through the gullies of Hawley, where bear and wild boar are known to have attacked van loads of kids. We will then climb up the rugged escarpment onto the high plateau of Plainfield, where we will traverse the frozen potato fields. Then onto Route 9 and down into the sleepy and quaint suburbs of Dalton, Pittsfield, and finally to Bousquet. Repeat after me."

We try, but when we get to the gullies of Hawley with the wild bears and boars it sounds like gibberish. So Phil chants one sentence at a time, making us repeat after him, like we're learning a foreign language.

"Guys" — he stops to lecture us — "the first rule of

racing is if you don't know where you're going, you can't get there."

"We don't have to know where we're going," a tiny voice challenges him. "You're driving."

"Who said that? Duncan, did you say that?"

Duncan shakes his head, trying not to laugh.

"Josh? Is that voice of dissension yours?"

"Nope," Josh yelps.

"It's me, Daddy." Molly's barely smiling. "You're being such a jerk."

"Ah." Phil's head sags as if he's been shot.

We all laugh.

"I just want these guys to be alert, Molly."

"Yup."

"Phil." His name comes flying out of my mouth even before I know I've said it.

"Yeah?"

"I have a question."

"A question? That's excellent, Sam. Without questions there can be no dialogue. Without dialogue there can be no learning. Without learning — "

"Daddy!"

"What's your question?"

"If we're going fifty and we have a head wind of ten, then wouldn't our air speed be sixty?"

Felix elbows me. "What is this, algebra class?"

"By golly, I think you're right. We better radio in the change. Felix, want to do that for us?"

"Not a chance."

"Duncan, hold the microphone for me."

Duncan holds his fist in front of Phil's mouth.

"Race team to Hawley Pothole Controllers. Come in, please." Phil flips on the radio and spins the dial until he gets static. "Ah, there you are. Our race team would like to make a correction. Our air speed is sixty miles per hour." He spins the knob of the radio so the van is filled with static. "Ah, thank you. Over and out." He turns off the radio, takes Duncan's hand, and pushes it away as if it's a microphone. "Okay, we're rolling now. See guys?" He looks at us in the rearview mirror. "If you don't know what you're doing you're going to get slowed down." He looks at us awhile and then lets his gaze drop and settles into just driving, and for the longest time no one says anything.

The van is quiet except for the drone of the exhaust as we climb out of the gullies of Hawley and up onto the high plateau of Plainfield. To the east there's an ice-covered lake, and along the far shore a row of birch trees. Behind the trees is the sun. Shafts of red light flood through the branches, bounce across the ice, and come hurtling through the van's windows, filling it with light. Leah's blond hair turns red. Phil's hat is on fire.

"Look!" Phil pounds the steering wheel with the palm of his hand. " 'The mountains and the hills before you shall break forth into singing.' I don't know who said that, but they're sure as hell right. Don't you see? This is what racing's all about. Sunrises and mountains singing."

Seven

WE PULL INTO the parking lot of Bousquet, wipe the condensation from the windows, and look out. The parking lot is empty except for the snowbanks and four cars. The mountain is empty. The chair lifts are still, the chairs hanging from their cables like frozen laundry. The lodge looks empty, too, except for the smoke snaking out of a chimney.

Duncan squints through the window. "You sure this is the place?"

"This is the place." Phil pulls on the emergency break and turns off the engine. "Remember what I've always told you, guys?"

No one says anything. He tells us so much, how could we possibly know what he's asking us to remember?

"About the early racer?" he asks.

No. We shake our heads and look at each other, wondering what he's going to say next.

"The early racer gets the turn." Phil laughs. No one else does.

"I don't get it, Phil." Felix is the only one who dares question Phil's sense of humor.

"Guys, do I tell you to turn before the gate or after the gate?"

"Before the gate," we all answer.

"And if you turn before the gate, is that called an early turn or a late turn?"

"An early turn."

"Need I say more?" He opens the door and freezing

cold air rushes over us. "The early racer gets the turn.
Let's go."

"I still don't get it."

"Me neither."

We grab our skis and poles and duffel bags and
lug them around the side of the lodge. The lodge is
made of two triangles balanced against each other.
Holding the triangles up are walls of glass brick. From
the mountain there's the roar of snow guns blowing
snow into piles along the edges of the main slope. We
lean our skis and poles against a wooden ski rack and
go inside.

"I still don't get it." Felix is standing next to Phil.
"The early skier gets the worm?"

Phil ignores him.

The inside of the lodge is a huge open room with a
cement floor covered with rows of brown picnic tables.
We take two in the middle and dump our bags on the
floor next to them. The walls that aren't glass are rough-
cut pine.

"There's no registration," Felix says, swinging his
head around like a bird. "This early bird doesn't get the
worm. We told you this was the wrong mountain, Phil."

"Will you can it, Felix?"

"Can the worms, guys."

"Felix."

"Phil."

Registration? Nobody told me anything about registration. What's registration? It definitely sounds like
something I should be worried about. "Phil, what's registration?"

"I'll see if they're open." Phil disappears up an open set of stairs at the end of the room.

"There's no registration. I tell you, it's the wrong mountain, Phil," Felix yells after him. He shakes his head as Phil disappears. "Geez, our coach missed his worm."

"What's registration?" I ask Louie, but he's heading across the room toward the video games. Josh follows him. The other guys sit at the table.

"What's registration?" I try again.

"It's nothing." Duncan unzips his brown parka.

"Yeah," I say, as if I know it's nothing.

"Take off your coat." Felix is sitting across the table. He pulls off his blue hat with the red and white pompom and scratches his scalp with both his hands. "All you do at registration is give them your name and they give you a racing bib."

"Oh." That doesn't sound too hard. I can give them my name. I sit down next to Duncan, unzip my parka, and look around. We're sitting next to the ski school counter. Hanging on the rough pine wall are framed pictures of ski intructors under a sign that says Get to Know Our Ski Instructors. I count them. There are forty-three framed pictures. I wonder how many weeks it would take to get to know all of them. Leah and Molly get up and wander off to the snack bar. I watch them standing under a pale, blue Pepsi sign. They each get a red paper cup of soda and a jelly doughnut. By the time they get back other racers and coaches are beginning to straggle into the lodge. I guess this is the place. We sit there until Phil whistles for us. We follow him upstairs, where at one end of the room there are folding tables, and women who look like mothers sitting behind them. They're all wearing turtlenecks and wool pants. Leah and Molly stand in one line, we stand in another. Leah comes away with a blue bib and the number five, Molly with a twenty, Duncan gets a red two, Felix is twelve, Josh twenty-four, Louie thirty-four. That's the order that they'll be racing in. I wonder what number I'll be. I step up to the lady and give her my name.

"Your USSA card, please."

"My what?"

"Your USSA card. In order for me to give you a bib you will have to give me your USSA card. At the end of the race you give us the bib and we give you back your card."

"Oh." I look around for Phil. "I don't have my USSA card." I say it with my head sideways.

"I beg your pardon?"

"I don't have my USSA card," I mumble, "but that's okay. I don't need a bib."

"You can't race without a bib."

"I don't need to race."

"Phil." I hear Molly calling her father.

"We'll take five dollars instead," the woman says.

"I don't have five dollars. I don't need to race."

Phil is suddenly standing next to me. "What's up?"

"I ah . . ."

"He doesn't have his card or five dollars."

"Here." Phil hands her a five-dollar bill.

I take the bib and fold it under my arm. There's a line of about ten racers behind me. I follow Phil downstairs.

The room is packed with racers taking something off or putting something on. I open my duffel bag and pull out my pants and boots. Everyone around me is in long underwear. I slip off my sweat pants, then pull on my blue and red slalom pants and my old-fashioned slalom sweater. The arms have padded ribbing from the shoulders to the wrists. Some of the ribbing is blue, some of it white. I pull the padding around from the back to the front of my arms. I take out my silk socks, smell them, wrinkle my nose, and pull them on. I look up occasionally. All the really good skiers are pulling their skintight nylon GS suits over their long johns. Even Molly has a GS suit. I wedge my feet into my yellow Technicas, adjust the black tongue, and crank the buckles so they're not too tight. The other guys pull their parkas and warm-up pants over their GS suits. Then they pull their bibs over their parkas. I pull my red warm-ups around my waist, Velcro the sides, pull the black belt through the silver buckle, and zip up the legs. Then I pull on my blue parka.

"Come on, guys." Phil is clapping his gloved hands. "We don't have all day."

"The lifts aren't even running," Louie mutters.

"We don't need lifts."

"Great," Louie mutters. "That's great."

"Come on, Sam." Phil fits the bib around my neck. "Remember, guys, when you're examining the course, two things. Always have your bib showing. And never ski through it. Snowplow and slipping only. You got it?"

"Got it." We nod.

"Good." He hands me my padded blue and yellow gloves, my blue and red hat, and my goggles. He zips my bag closed. "You guys ready?"

"Yeah."

Sort of.

"You look ready. You look like a band of Ninja warriors ready to take on the world."

"Ninja warriors?" Felix asks. "So you think we're going to ski like a bunch of turtles, huh?"

Eight

OUTSIDE, THE SKY is ice blue. The sun is shining somewhere, but not here. The air catches me by surprise. It's still early-morning cold. We snap into our bindings and start after Phil. Up ahead of us a snowcat is grooming the snow. The driver is drinking a cup of coffee inside the red cab. Black diesel exhaust is snarling straight up into the blue sky. Behind the cat, hanging from yellow hydraulics, trails a black snow groomer. It grinds up the old snow and lays down packed powder in tiny diamond-shaped patterns.

"Wrong wax," Felix yells. "My skis are sticking. I got the wrong damn wax."

"Me too!" the rest of us yell. Our skis, instead of gliding, grip the snow like studded snow tires.

"Come on, guys," Phil yells over his shoulder."Any jerk can complain."

"Right. Thanks, Phil, for your understanding," we mutter under our breaths.

We ski past the blue chair lift, past the towrope and the beginner's slope. Sometimes we skate. Mostly we double-pole. When it gets steep we roll our ankles and walk on the inside edge of our skis. We climb up underneath the yellow chair lift, the empty chairs dangling in the blue sky.

"What's your number?" Louie pants next to me.

"What's yours?" I pant back.

"Thirty-four," he pants. "I'm all set. As long as I ski once in the top forty, I'll get invited to the Tri-State Championships. I made it last year. So I know I'll make it this year. What's your number?" He's panting in my face.

"I don't know. I forgot to look."

"Yeah, right." He laughs as if I just told a joke. "You probably got a high number. They put all the lousy racers at the back of the pack." He reaches over my shoulder and grabs the bib, pulling it around so that he can read it.

"Ha." He laughs again and a green piece of snot shoots out of his nose. "You're ninety-nine. The last guy to go. You poor jerk. You know how icy and shitty the course is for the last guy? No point in even racing." He lets go of my bib and I slide backward, almost falling. I catch myself with my left hand and watch him skate off after the others.

"Hey, guys, you know what number Sam is? Ninety-nine. That means there are ninety-eight guys ahead of him. The poor jerk's in the back of the pack."

I stay where I am, watching them climb over the knoll and disappear around one of the chair lift towers. He's right. There isn't any point in my racing. I should have stayed home. I didn't even want to come. I look back at the lodge. A few racers are putting on their skis. I turn around and start gliding down the hill, wiping little flecks of ice away from my eyes with the back of my glove. I'll wait in the lodge for them. I've got a couple of quarters. I can play videos. I pop out of my bindings, lean my skis and poles in the rack, unbuckle my boots, and start for the door of the lodge.

I walk straight into a pair of arms. I don't even have to look up to know who they belong to. The arms wrap around me, ski poles dangling from them, skis on both sides of my boots. And I just stand there crying in his arms, my chest heaving, my throat aching. I wish I were dead. I try to get away, but Phil won't let go and all I can see is the red fabric of his parka. He waits until I'm finished and then puts his hands on my shoulders and looks straight at me. I can see myself in his goggles: a little kid with blond hair and freckles, blue eyes, and a face smeared with tears.

"You know we all have to start sometime, and in skiing the only place they let us start is in the back. That's where we all started. You don't have to be ashamed of starting there. That's just the way it's done. It doesn't matter for one second that that's where you started. What matters is where you finish. And I'm not talking about today's race. I'm talking about one year from now, two years from now, three years from now. I'm talking about what you decide to do with skiing. I don't know how good you're going to be, Sam, and I don't usually make predictions, but I'm going to make an exception today. Today, I'm predicting you're going to be a good one."

"Yeah, right." I push away from him and try to hide my smile.

"Time will tell. In any case, I have something else to tell you."

"What?"

"The first race is one of the toughest, and the sooner it's behind you the better. Today all I expect you to do is show up."

"You mean not race?"

"No, I want you to race. I want you to start, but all I want you to do is ski the course like practice, and whatever happens, happens."

"What if I fall?"

"If you fall you fall."

*————— **Nine** —————*

BY THE TIME we catch up to the others, the yellow chair lift is running and racers are gliding over our heads, the bottom of their skis like wings.

"The lift's going, Phil." Felix points at the yellow chairs with his ski pole. "We'll just ski down and get on, right?"

"Wrong." Phil hardly stops to catch his breath before continuing to climb.

"Phil," Felix and Leah shout. Louie hits the snow with his pole.

The rest of us start after Phil. We hike up to the finish line, a red stripe painted in the snow. On both ends, standing on knee-high tripods, are the electronic eyes for the automatic timer. There's an orange mesh fencing around and behind the finish area to keep us from crashing into the crowds. Behind the fencing is a white leader board with our names printed in blue. Above the finish line the GS course of red and blue gates meanders up the white slope.

We cross the red line and hike up between the first pair of blue gates and up through the first pair of red ones. Every few gates Phil stops and tells us exactly how he wants us to ski that section of the course. Other racers and their coaches are beginning to snowplow down the mountain. We're the only team hiking. By the time we get to the steeps we're all sweating, our parkas and warm-up pants are unzipped, our hats are in our pockets, and our goggles are drooping around our necks. I try not to fall as we sidestep up the last part of the steeps. The mountain calls it packed powder, but what it really is is a two-inch layer of granular snow covering a glacier of sheer ice. It'll only be a half hour before the packed powder is scraped off, leaving only the ice.

When we finally get to the top, we stand there sweating and breathing hard, our gloves cupped over the top of our poles, our armpits hooked over our gloves. Half standing, half hanging from our poles, we gaze down the mountain. The course is filled with over a hundred racers and looks more like a brightly colored city street at rush hour than a race course. I try to follow the alternating blue and red gates as they snake down to the finish, red, blue, red, wondering, How am I going to remember let alone make all those turns? Because it's too much to consider, my eyes wander out over the city of Pittsfield. I have never been to a ski mountain that was this close to the downtown. It's as if Bousquet were in the parking lot of city hall, the rooftops and gutters, the steeples and fire escapes are that close. Even the hangarlike buildings and gray smokestacks of General Electric shooting white soot into the sky seem close. To the north, dwarfing everything, is a huge brown mountain. The way the early-morning sunlight just touches the top of the mountain makes it look like something that might have been alive thousands of years ago.

"Okay." Phil clears his throat. "Let's go through it once more."

We snowplow down through the course behind Phil, who takes the opportunity to repeat everything he said on the way up. Then we get in line for the yellow chair. Louie ends up with Phil, I end up with Josh. We glide in front of the chair. The attendant holds the back so that the seat dips under us. We sit down. Our skis glide on the snow and then the chair lifts us into the air and swings us up toward the first yellow tower. We pull the safety bar down.

"I wouldn't want to be Louie right now." Josh looks off into the woods. "Phil's going to give it to him. He was wrong to say that stuff. It's just that he's not sure of himself, you know?"

"Yeah," I say, but I don't know.

"You'll be okay, Sam. Just don't worry about it. It doesn't help. Believe me, I speak from experience."

———— Ten ————

I LOOK DOWN at the course from the chair. The panels on the gates are fluttering in the breeze that ripples down the mountain as the sun climbs higher in the sky. A few racers are still on the course, trying to figure out the most difficult sections. Pushed off to the side of the trail are snow guns, their stainless steel muzzles pointing toward the woods. We pass over the start, where a crowd of racers and coaches is gathering. A current of adrenaline zaps through me and my leg jerks so that my knee kicks the safety bar up.

"Whoa, we don't get off here, dude." Josh pushes the bar back down.

"Yeah." I try to smile.

"Got to relax."

"Right." Relax, relax, I tell myself as we glide up over a mogul field to where the mountain flattens out. We come to a wooden tower that looks like a ski jump, lift our safety bar, ski down the slide, and follow Phil and the others through the mogul field. We take a lot of air jumping from one mogul to the next. Josh and Louie do spread–eagles. Felix and Duncan do helicopters. They jump off one mogul, spin completely around in midair, and land on another mogul. I do a back scratch. In midair I bring my skis behind me until they touch my back so that it looks as if I'm flying through the air on my knees. The only hard part of these jumps is to get your skis underneath you before you land. We spray to a stop at the start of the course, where a crowd of girl racers and their coaches are scraping skis, adjusting bindings, putting on or taking off parkas, tying their bibs.

Phil snaps out of his skis and sticks them in the snow to the side of the trail.

"Leah and Molly, time to get ready. Guys, take one more run, but make it quick."

Duncan and Felix take off. Double-poling and skating, they cut over to the next trail. The rest of us follow. They get into a tuck until they hit the steeps, where they start cranking hard, tight GS turns. We follow in their tracks. At the bottom of the mountain there's no line, and we glide onto the chair lift without stopping. Halfway up, we see Leah on course. She's skiing stiff and safe, but she's taking a good line. We yell and cheer, whacking our poles together, as if our cheering will make her go faster. When we get to the top, we blitz through the mogul field, and by the time we get to the start, Molly's in the starting gate. Phil is right beside her, rubbing her shoulders, whispering encouragement. On the other side the starter is giving the command.

"Molly," we chant, "Molly." She lifts her head slightly so she can see us through her goggles, smiles, kicks her feet in the air, and is gone.

"Go, Molly," Phil shouts after her.

We click our poles and shout until we can't see her anymore. Phil starts over to us.

We smile at him. "She looked good, Phil."

"She slid out some on the fourth gate. You guys will have to watch it; it's steep and it's icy and it falls away. You're going to have to ride that downhill ski. You understand?"

We nod. I understand what he's saying. It's just doing it that's hard. Whenever I feel my downhill ski slipping away I want to get off it and stand on the uphill ski. But Phil wants us to throw our hip out over the slipping downhill ski so that our weight will force it to carve through the ice. It makes sense the way he explains it. It just doesn't make sense when I'm out there and the ski is slipping. It's like being in a canoe that's tipping over and being told to throw my weight to the side that's sinking. If I did that I'd immediately roll over. In skiing my brain wants to use the same logic. It wants me to stay away from the side that's going down.

Phil claps his gloves. "Time to warm up. Take off your skis and run up into the mogul field.

We snap out of our bindings.

He claps again. "Hup! Hup!"

We hup up through the moguls, kicking the hard plastic toes of our boots into the ice. When we slow down Phil yells at us to keep going. So we climb higher, our lungs burning, and we don't stop until we hear his whistle. Then we turn around and ski down on the soles of our boots. When we get back, he has us stretch. We spread our boots as far apart as we can and touch the snow with our elbows. We push against the trunks of trees. We sit on the snow and pretend to hurdle over hurdles. We do fifteen sit-ups and ten pushups. Then he has us scrape the bottoms of our skis. There are only two scrapers, so I wait for Duncan as he turns over one of his skis, and holding the clear red plastic scraper in both hands, starts scraping. He starts at the tip and goes down the ski, overlapping his strokes. He pants as he scrapes.

"Get the wax thin," he mumbles as he gets to the end of the ski.

"So the ski will be fast," Felix adds as he finishes his ski and wipes the sweat off his brow.

"Hey, Duncan," Louie calls from where he's standing.

"Yeah."

"Look at Reich over there, talking to Durell."

"Yeah."

"He's a got a new jacket."

"So?"

"Look at it."

I look over. I've heard of both Reich and Durell but I've never seen them. They're two of the top skiers in the state. Sometimes Duncan beats them, but usually Reich's first or second. Durell is Duncan's age. He's the tall one in the green GS suit. Reich is my age. His sisters are on the U.S. ski team, and in the summer he trains with them while they train with the team, which means that he trains with the U.S. ski team. In case we don't know that, he's wearing a blue parka with huge red letters on the back that read U.S.A. Ski Team.

"Give me a break." Felix spits in the snow. "What's he doing with that jacket?"

"Intimidating," Louie answers.

Felix's lower lip pouts. "He's not so good."

Duncan nods slowly. "Yeah."

"I'm going to beat him today," Louie announces.

Felix and Duncan laugh. "Right."

"Just watch."

By the time they finish scraping their skis and cranking up the bindings to the highest din, the last girl is in the start. We watch her go. She skids through four gates, falls as she enters the steeps, slides through a red gate on her hips, and disappears into a crowd of racers standing on the side of the course.

"Bib numbers one, two, three, four, five," a guy in a gray parka with a clipboard starts yelling. "Line up. We'll be starting in three minutes. Three minutes. Numbers six, seven, eight, nine, ten, get ready, please."

Three minutes. I'm not ready. Another jolt of adrenaline surges through me. I haven't even scraped my skis or tightened my bindings. Three minutes. Then I remember that I'm ninety-nine, and for the first time since I got that number I'm happy. Ninety-nine in ski racing has to be like infinity. It'll never come. I take a breath and relax. I watch Duncan and Felix unzip their warm-up pants down the sides of their legs. They unsnap them at the waist, and the pants peel off like the skin of a dragonfly. They unzip their parkas and throw them on their warm-ups. Duncan is wearing a silver gray GS suit. Felix is wearing dark blue. They help each other tie their bibs so the red numbers show on both the back and the front. Then Felix puts his blue parka back on.

"Number one," the guy with the clipboard shouts. Number one slides into the starting gate. Duncan skates slowly to the start and stops about five yards away. Phil is right next to him, his arm around his shoulder, talking into his ear. I go down to the third gate and look up at the start. The sun is rising over the mogul field and I have to squint to see the first racer as he skis straight at me.

"This guy sucks," someone says. I turn and look. It's Louie. "I can beat him."

"Yeah." I nod. When I turn back, the racer has disappeared into the steeps. I turn and squint into the sun. Duncan's in the start. In his silver suit he looks like a Polaroid picture before it has developed. I watch him put his poles in front of the starting wand. Then the starter taps him on the arm, and Duncan kicks the back of his skis in the air and swings through the start and straight toward us.

"Not bad," Louie says in my ear. This time I don't turn.

"Go, Duncan," I shout. His turns are strong and powerful and he looks faster than the first racer. I watch him disappear into the steeps and then reappear in the flats. I watch him until he's no larger than a silver dollar rolling across the snow, and then I lose him. I forget to watch the next nine racers. I just stand there thinking how I'm going to run the course. I wake up in time to watch Felix flash out of the sun. He's fast and as smooth as his dark blue GS suit. His upper body is absolutely still while his legs swing and bend at each turn. Then I watch Josh in his green suit, then Louie in his bright yellow suit, and then the racers' bib numbers begin to blur and time stands still and speeds up and suddenly

I'm watching racers in the fifties, then the sixties. That's still a long way from ninety-nine, I tell myself, and I don't panic until Phil shouts my name.

——————— Eleven ———————

I CLIMB UP to him, kicking my boots into the ice, one leg at a time. I know I'm moving. I know I'm getting closer to him. I just can't feel my legs. It's as if they belong to someone else.

"Sam. Twenty more and you're up, kid." He's clapping his gloves. I recognize the thudding sound. "Have you scraped your skis?"

I shake my head no. He hands me a scraper. I kneel down next to my skis, turn them over, and try to do what Duncan did. I press as hard as I can, pulling the scraper from the tip of the ski to the tail. A thin film of wax curls out from underneath the scraper. My thumbs and fingers grow numb from the cold. Phil's shadow passes over me.

"Good, Sam." He kneels down next to me and takes the scraper from my hand. "You want to pull it a little quicker and a little harder." Ribbons of wax peel off the scraper. "See?" He turns the ski over. "The extra wax will just slow you down." He scrapes the other ski.

"Thanks," I mumble when he finishes.

"Now let's tighten your bindings. We don't want you popping out of these bindings on your first turn." He takes a screwdriver out of his pack and turns the din clockwise until it won't turn anymore. He does the other binding, and when he stands up he straightens himself by pushing his right fist into the small of his back.

"Ninety through ninety-nine, come get in line," the man with the clipboard shouts. Adrenaline jolts through me again.

"That's me." I start stepping into my bindings.

"Wait." Phil slaps my leg. "Lift up your right boot." He leans over and scrapes off the mound of snow on the sole of my boot. Then I snap it into my bindings. He does the other boot and I snap into the other ski. I lean over and crank the buckles of my boots as tight as they'll go. I unzip my red warm-ups and my blue parka and throw them to the side of the trail. Phil helps me tie the bib around my red sweater. I slip my gloves through the leather straps of my poles and close my hands around the grips. Adrenaline rippling through my skin makes me feel something.

"Phil, I got to go."

"You got time. There are nine ahead of you. Relax, you got plenty of time."

"I mean I have to go. You know, go."

"You mean you got to pee?"

I nod. "Yeah."

"Forget it. You don't have that kind of time. You'll have to wait until you get to the lodge."

"Ah, geez." Stupidly, I look up and down the mountain for the door to a bathroom.

He pats me on the shoulder. "Let's get in line."

I skate to where ninety-six through ninety-eight are

waiting. Ninety-eight turns and smiles at me nervously. I smile back. I could be looking into a mirror.

"Good luck," he says.

"Yeah. You too."

Phil is talking into my ear. "All I want is for you to finish. To go through this course and to finish. That's all you need to do, do you understand?"

I nod my head.

"Nothing fast. No world records. Just finish."

"Yeah." I watch ninety-eight leave the gate. He looks scared and stiff, as if he wishes he were somewhere else, doing something else. God, please don't let me look like that. Please, even if I'm scared don't let me look like that.

"Ninety-nine, come in and get yourself ready; you have twenty seconds."

"Have a good run, Sam." Phil rubs my back and shoulders. "You're just going to finish. Just going to get this one race under your belt. No world records. No top-twenty finish. Just get this one under your belt."

"Ninety-nine, the starting command will be 'Ready, set, go.' After I say go you have ten seconds."

"Ten seconds to what?"

"To go, young man, to go."

I put my poles over the purple starting wand. I've done this in practice. There are two big holes from the other racers' poles. I try to find a place to put the tips of my poles so they won't slip into the holes. Then I look down the course. I see the first gate a little to my right. Then the blue one off to the left.

"Racer . . . ready . . . set . . . go."

"Just finish, Sam," I hear Phil yell. "Just finish."

I don't kick up the back of my skis. I just slide through the wand and half skate, half glide toward the first gate. I'm thinking how I have to be early for the turn when the gate disappears and I'm surrounded by white fog. I glance quickly down the mountain for the other gates, but they're gone. Oh, Christ. Another jolt of adrenaline. I want to stop, but Phil's at the top yelling at me to just finish. I look down in front of my skis. There are ruts in the snow carved by the first one hundred and forty-eight racers. I can see them clearly if I bend low over my skis. I follow the ruts, my skis chattering. I turn when they turn, go straight when they go straight.

"Go, Sam," I hear Felix and Duncan yelling at the edges of the fog.

"Go, Sam." Molly and Leah.

I make my next turn and suddenly the fog is lifted and I can see the gates. I'm halfway through the course! I made it through the steeps. I take the next gate and the next. I can't believe how much easier it is to race when you can see where you're going.

"Go, Sam." The voices are staying with me. "Go."

I can actually see the finish, white flags fluttering in the wind. Just a couple of gates left. I tuck the way Phil told us, but I don't roll my skis right. I kind of skid through the red gate, but straighten out in time for the blue and then the red finish line. I throw my poles over the line to trip the timer and, nearly falling, slide to a stop. When I get my balance I slowly glide out through the opening in the orange mesh.

"Way to go, Sam." Felix is standing there, a big smile

on his face. The other guys are standing next to him.

"Thanks," I pant as I unbuckle my boots.

"Time for racer number ninety-nine is 58.43."

"Good time, Sam," Duncan and Molly say together.

"Thanks." I suddenly feel beads of sweat dripping down my back. I shiver. "I would have done better if I didn't have to ski through the fog."

"What fog?" Felix asks.

"On the top of the mountain."

"What are you talking about? There wasn't any fog."

"When I was racing."

"There wasn't any fog when you were racing." Felix laughs as if I have just told a joke. "That was just nerves. You were just fogging out with nerves.

"Nerves?" I smile stupidly.

"Hey." Duncan taps me on the shoulder. "Fog or no fog, you skied great for your first race."

"Thanks." A warm feeling alternates with the shivers, kind of like sweet and sour.

"I'm starving." Duncan turns and starts gliding slowly down the slope toward the lodge. "Let's eat."

"Yeah." Leah and Molly and Josh start after him.

"You coming, Foggy Mountain?" Felix asks.

"Yeah, I'm coming." But first I look up the mountain. Instead of fog, there's only the brightly colored course against the white snow and blue sky. And skiing out of the brightness, heading straight for me, is Phil.

✳————— Twelve —————✳

THE ODOR OF dried sweat, like stale flowers, fills the van. Phil turns on the radio as we bump along. It's over. I close my eyes and for the first time today I feel that my body belongs to me. My legs, my arms. On the mountain everything felt disconnected. I open and close my right hand. It's over. I finished my first race, I didn't crash, I didn't die, and I'm on my way home. It's a good feeling. The end of a race day is definitely better than the beginning. It's okay to be thirteen and going home on a Sunday afternoon. But I'm tired. Everyone is tired and half asleep. I wonder what I'll remember about this race. Memories are strange. They are like dreams that you end up filling in with detail because they get foggy. I definitely don't want to remember the fog.

"Felix?" I nudge him with my elbow.

"What?" He half yawns, half growls.

"Nothing."

"You woke me up for nothing?"

"Can you explain something?"

"What?"

"How many more races do we have?"

"Two."

"What do I have to do to make the Tri-State Championships?"

Louie turns around in the seat in front of us and stares at me with a stupid grin. "Ski better."

"Shut up, Louie." Felix kicks the back of the seat. "He's not talking to you."

Phil turns off the radio. "What's going on?"

"Sam wants to know if he can make the championships."

"Sam? Sam, I don't even want you thinking about the championships this year."

"See?" Louie snarls.

"Will you shut up?" Felix snaps. "I'm talking to Phil. Phil, supposing he finished in the top forty at least once. He'd qualify, right?"

"For what?"

"The championships."

"Yeah, but he doesn't need that kind of pressure, Felix."

"I'm just supposing. What did Sam get today?"

"Seventieth after his second run."

"That's not bad for his first race."

"Yeah." Duncan echoes. "To go from ninety-ninth to seventieth means he beat twenty-nine guys."

Louie laughs. "Yeah, but he still has a long way to go."

"Louie." Phil looks at him in the rearview mirror.

"Yeah?"

"I remember a kid whose first race wasn't so hot."

"That's because no one told me."

"That's because it never occurred to anyone to tell a kid not to ski through the course backward."

"I got confused."

"So you can appreciate what Sam did today. He could have gotten confused."

"Yeah, well, there was the fog on the first run." Felix nudges me in the ribs.

"What?" Phil turns the radio back on.

"Nothing. Just a little joke between me and Sam." Then he whispers in my ear, "You can beat those guys. If Louie can beat them they've got to be just a bunch of turkeys."

Louie makes a fist. "Watch it, Felix."

"You think I'm scared of a turkey killer."

"Felix!" Phil shouts.

"Phil."

"Put a bag over your head or something. It's been a long day."

"Right." He pulls his hat down over his face. "How's this?"

"As long as your mouth is covered."

"Mmphhh."

"Felix?" I whisper through the wool. "When's our next race?"

"Two weeks. How come a kid who's taking algebra in seventh grade can't remember a race schedule?"

"I don't know."

He leans his head against the window. "Do me a favor. Let me go to sleep before you get me into any more trouble, okay?"

"Okay." I close my eyes. Three races. Two weeks until the next race. Fortieth. I say it to myself like it's an equation. How can I come in fortieth in one of the next two races? It's like trying to solve a calculus problem when all I know is basic algebra. It can't be done. The van swerves around a bend. I open my eyes. Headlights veer past us. Already it's night.

——————— Thirteen ———————

IT'S STILL DARK and snowing lightly. It's so quiet, I can hear the snow ticking on the sleeves of my parka. We stand on the side of the road. Seven o'clock in the morning. Usually I have to run down from the house to catch the bus. But this morning I woke early and couldn't go back to sleep. I stand there in my old running shoes, writing numbers in the snow with my toe, working on an old problem. Bo is staring off into space. Our breaths are curled over our heads.

The bus comes roaring around the curve, its headlights flashing straight at us. A cloud of exhaust and snow swirls around it like steam around a space shuttle when it blasts off. Except for the yellow blinking lights, it doesn't look like it's going to stop. With its engine roaring, the brakes hiss and the bus skids to a stop in front of us. The door swings open. We climb up and even before we can turn down the aisle, Salvador guns the engine and we're whining down the road.

"Salvador," Bo scolds. "You want to kill us."

"Sit. Sit," he says in his pidgin English. "Sit down, please. This bus is express."

We're the last ones Salvador picks up. After us he figures he's got to make up time for all the kids he had to wait for. Salvador drives by the clock. Every day, rain, sleet, or snow, he tries to beat his best time. I pull my way down the aisle using the back of the seats like ski poles. I find a window seat, drop my book bag on the floor, and throw myself against the window.

Bo sits down next to me. "He's crazy. One of these days he's going to kill us."

"We definitely could use seat belts."

"We definitely could use life insurance."

I watch the scenery whip by. We race along the side of the Deerfield River and the Boston and Maine railroad tracks. A freight train is coming in the opposite direction. I'm glad the tracks and the road don't cross. We whip past each other, the width of an eighteenth-century graveyard between us, past a trailer park and onto Route 2. The road is clearer here and Salvador can really make time. We're doing sixty-five when we roar past the Christmas Tree Farm. The wind from our passing is like a hurricane through the trees' branches. We pull out in the passing lane and flash past a Toyota pickup. This kind of speed has an unusual effect on kids. We sit in our seats and don't dare move until we get to school. We're the best-behaved bus of all the routes and the principal loves Salvador.

Salvador was never supposed to be a school bus driver. He was never supposed to know how to drive. In fact, he was never supposed to be in America, but here he is whipping us down the highway at almost seventy miles an hour. Every kid on the bus knows that Salvador was born in the Amazon, the son of a Stone Age tribe. How he ever got to Massachusetts to drive a school bus is beyond me. I wonder what the odds are of a Stone Age kid from the Amazon growing up to be a school bus driver in Massachusetts. Probably about the same as me making it into the top forty.

———— Fourteen ————

FIRST PERIOD IS algebra. We're in a small room with black and silver pipes hanging from a ceiling and white paint peeling. There are a couple of windows by the pipes, but they're small and dirty. So the lights are always on. There are twenty-five of us.

I sit in the front row copying the homework assignment. Mr. Reilly is sitting at his desk. He's bald but he's not old, and even when he gets old he won't be old. He's got a mustache to make up for his baldness. He always wears a sweater and black-frame glsses. I finish copying the assignment, then look around the classroom at the old periodic table, the papier-mâché dinosaurs, stuff from his science courses. I like algebra. Most of the kids are ninth and tenth graders. Felix and Duncan are in the back. They sit as far away from Mr. Reilly as they can, praying they won't be asked to go to the board.

Mr. Reilly clears his throat, but before he can say anything, we start taking out last night's homework. The room is filled with the sound of books opening, papers unfolding, and nervous coughing in the back of the room.

"Problem one. Who would like to do it?"

I raise my hand. I know that problems only get tougher and I know I'm going to get called on, so why not get credit while doing the easiest?

"Sam."

I start to give the answer.

"Why don't you do it on the board?"

I pick up a piece of chalk and write the problem on the faded blackboard. Copying my work, I divide both sides of the equation by eight so that X will stand alone. I write down the answer.

"Good. Everybody understand what Sam did? Felix? Duncan? Can you see the board from back there?

"Oh, yes."

"Ah-huh."

"Good. Felix, you want to do problem seven?"

"What about two?"

"I thought seven was your lucky number."

"I never said that."

"What's your lucky number, then?"

"Ah." I can tell he's wishing he had a hall pass. "I don't have a lucky number."

Mr. Reilly smiles. He holds his right elbow in his left hand, his right hand rubbing his chin as if he's confused. He's like a cat with a mouse. I turn around and look at Felix. He's kind of smiling, too, a mouselike smile.

"In that case, for the sake of keeping things moving, do number seven even if it's not your favorite number. The blackboard is all yours. And while he's working on that, Duncan, why don't you think about number ten?"

"Yes, sir."

Felix rubs his finger in the chalk dust, picks up a piece of chalk, and starts to write the problem out in long hand.

"Sam," he whispers into his armpit.

"Yeah?"

"What do I do?"

I turn to see where Mr. Reilly is. He's sitting in the next to last row between Rebecca and Francesca.

"You divide," I whisper back.

"Divide what?"

"Divide one thousand three hundred and twenty-six by point forty-seven."

He writes out the equation and begins the long division. I give him a little help. "Three," I whisper. "And move the decimal."

"Sam." Mr. Reilly's voice is soft and high. It makes me think of flowers and birds.

"Yes." I turn around in my seat. I can feel my face turning red.

"You're developing quite a sunburn sitting up in the front row. Is it too bright for you up there?"

"No, sir."

"Good. Felix seems to be having problems with a wandering decimal. Could you show him where it goes?"

"Yes, sir." I get out of my seat and point. My finger leaves a damp spot on the board.

"Jerk," Felix hisses. "Why didn't you tell me?"

"I told you." My mouth is closed tighter than a ventriloquist's.

"Thank you, Sam. Felix, do you understand how it works now?"

"Yup."

"Good. Before you go on I want to tell all of you a brief story. Stop me anytime if you have any questions. Once upon a time there was an algebra class of twenty-five students, not unlike this class, that went to this pretty hip high school."

A half smile curls along the side of Felix's mouth. The rest of us quickly look at each other.

"One day their teacher, who was a fair and decent man, gave them an assignment. Some of the students, who were bright, did the assignment. Other students, who it must be understood were equally bright, decided they couldn't be bothered. The next day the students came to school and the teacher soon realized who had done their homework and who hadn't. He made tiny marks in a little book. Not unlike this one." He holds up a maroon grading book. "Later in the period a surprise quiz was given. To no one's surprise, except perhaps their own, the students who hadn't bothered to do their homework did poorly while the other students got decent grades. Now, this wasn't the first time this had happened. Is everybody following this story, so far?"

We all nod our heads.

"Good. Now I want everybody to clear their desk and take out a clean piece of paper."

Half the class moans. Mr. Reilly goes to the board and erases Felix's problem. He writes the following equation:

"Homework + X = Success."

"What is this, a quiz?" someone asks.

"Solve the equation for X." He wipes the chalk dust on his pants' legs.

"Is this a trick question?" someone asks.

"Only if you have a trick answer."

Fifteen

MOST AFTERNOONS after school we get a ride to the mountain with Ken. Ken is the all-purpose man at school. When something breaks, Ken fixes it. If the lines need to be put down on the field an hour before a game, Ken puts them down. If the furnace breaks down and the pipes freeze in the middle of the night, Ken gets out of bed, fixes the furnace, and thaws out the pipes. If kids need a ride to the mountain, chances are Ken will drive them. Ken's as skinny as the cigarettes he smokes. He always wears the same green-checkered Irish hat with the brim pulled down over his forehead and turtleneck shirts that make him look like a priest. And he's always smiling, as if he's just a won a fortune at the dog races. He never goes anywhere without his dog, Oscar. Oscar is a miniature dog with a squashed-in face. Kids joke that it's from chasing parked cars, but never in front of Ken.

If we start bugging Ken for a ride before lunch chances are by the time school's out, he'll take us over in his old suburban. His suburban is such a wreck I don't know how it passes inspection. When driving down the road it shakes and rattles and wanders back and forth across the yellow line.

Today Ken is giving five of us a ride. Felix, Duncan, and I are in the middle seat. Bo and his friend Miranda are in the back. Ken is wrestling with the steering wheel while Oscar is at his shoulder barking at cars going in the opposite direction. I can barely hear him bark because the muffler's broken. We roar across the Deerfield River, over the train tracks, past the horse farm, and into Thunder Mountain's parking lot. We bounce over the ruts and up along the driveway that curves beneath the pines to the back of the main lodge. We stop between the lodge and the race shack and scramble out, sucking fresh air into our lungs. Duncan climbs onto the roof and starts handing down skis and ski bags. I suck in another breath of fresh air and can't help smelling the pines and the diesel fuel from the snowcats. These are the same smells as when I started skiing with Mary ten years ago. If I close my eyes I can almost see her pulling me, a three-year-old kid, to the race shack.

"Yo, Sam, take these." I look up and Duncan is passing me my skis. I take them and lean them against a pine tree. Duncan jumps down and Ken fires up the suburban.

"Thanks, Ken." We wave and give him plenty of clearance. Ken doesn't wave back but pulls between two huge pines and cuts the engine.

"Time for a cup of hot java and a cigarette." He locks the suburban as if somebody would actually steal it and comes walking toward us. He carries Oscar, hooked over his forearm, the way a ventriloquist carries his dummy. I open the door for them. They walk over to the snack bar while we go upstairs to change.

It's a large, open room with a cathedral ceiling held up by posts and beams painted black. Hanging from the rafters are yellow, purple, and orange flags with white designs of snowflakes and skis. We spread our stuff out over a couple of the varnished tables, take off our pants, and pull on our long johns. We try not to look when Miranda takes off her skirt and pulls on her long johns, but I can't help noticing how smooth her legs are. I quickly pull on my ski socks so that I don't say something dumb, hoping nobody noticed I noticed.

"Nice legs." Felix smiles.

Miranda doesn't say anything. She just scowls at him as she pulls up her long underwear around her waist. Bo doesn't say anything either. He just hits Felix hard with a right jab.

"For Chrissakes." Felix grabs his shoulder. "It was a joke."

"Right." Bo rubs his fist sort of like it hurts and sort of like he's getting ready to hit him again.

"All right." Felix grabs his stuff and starts for the stairs. "I apologize. I apologize."

"Geez, Bo." I feel guilty, as if it was my fault for thinking what I was thinking. "You didn't have to kill him."

"He's got to learn not to act like an animal," Bo mutters.

"Yeah." I pull on my gloves. "You okay, Miranda?"

"Yes." She pulls on her turquoise parka.

I pull on my hat and then for no reason at all I say, "That Ken is something. You think he's going to buy Oscar a coffee?"

I can tell no one is listening because nobody answers me. So I just stand there and wait. Bo helps Miranda put on her turquoise ear band by standing still while she looks at herself in his goggles. When she's all set we troop downstairs, our ski boots pounding the steps like thunder.

Ken is standing by the ski racks, sipping steaming coffee from a large Styrofoam cup. Oscar's at his feet, chewing on half a doughnut. We click into our bindings, wave good-bye to Ken and Oscar, and skate over to the green chair lift. Duncan goes up by himself. Bo goes up with Miranda and I go up with Felix. We don't say anything. We just sit there riding up the mountain, our poles dangling from our wrists, the safety bar up in the air, our skis crossing like swords. It's warm, in the twenties, and in the late-afternoon sun there are long shadows everywhere across the snow. I turn around and look over the valley. It doesn't look real from up here. In fact, it looks like a toy village a kid has made for his train set. Everything looks miniature. The lodge, the parking lot, the silver train tracks along the river, the cold, green-brown river flecked with ice, the cars crossing the stone bridge, the clapboard houses with smoke curling out of their chimneys, and the snow-coverd fields between the village and the mountains rolling back to the horizon.

I turn around and moan. I don't know why I moan. It just escapes from me. I feel overwhelmed. I don't know if it's the view, or what Felix said, or Bo punching Felix, or Miranda's skin. I don't know. Maybe it's all of them. Maybe it's none of them. Maybe it's because I don't know that I moan again.

"What's the matter with you?" Felix hits my leg with his ski pole.

"Ouch." I rub my knee.

"You sound like a sick cow."

"Sorry."

"I'm the one that should be moaning. I can't believe how hard your brother punches."

"Yeah." I nod. "That boy can punch."

"My arm feels like it's going to fall off."

"Well, I wouldn't take your sweater off tonight."

"Why?"

"Just in case."

"Just in case what?"

"Just in case it does fall off."

"Thanks."

We get to the top of the mountain and slide off the chair. We glide away from the lift to the side of the trail where the ski patrol keep their red sleds. We bend down and crank our boot buckles tight, adjust our goggles, and slip our gloves through the leather straps of our poles. We look at Bo to see which trail we're going to take. Bo looks at Miranda.

"The Sunrise?" she asks.

The Sunrise is an intermediate trail. Not hard. Not easy. But it can get icy and full of moguls in the chute. Bo double-poles to the head of the trail. We follow him. He takes off skating and double-poling to pick up speed. Miranda is right behind him and we're right behind her. The top of Sunrise is just steep enough to pick up speed if you tuck. We tuck. Our poles under our arms, our elbows resting on our knees, we cruise through the upper Sunrise. No turns. No stopping. Just tucking. And when we hit the lip of the chute, we're flying. Bo goes off first, staying in his tuck. Miranda stands up and slows down so her skis stay on the snow. We come whipping past her, first Duncan, then Felix, then me. Duncan and I straighten up in the air, but Felix holds his tuck and soars through the air like an eagle. I land on top of a mogul on my inside ski and lean so far back I almost fall.

My rear bounces off a mogul, and as I pull myself upright I fly off a second mogul. Somehow I land on both skis. I make a couple of quick slalom turns and stop at the cutoff. Bo, Felix, and Duncan are long gone. Miranda skis over to me and stops.

"You see that?" I ask.

"You are a jerk, Sam," she scolds. "You guys are going to end up sticking out of trees if you keep skiing like that."

"You didn't like my form?" I ask, but she doesn't answer. She's already started down the cutoff, skiing under control. I follow her. Skiing slowly I half watch her, half stare at the late-afternoon sun coming sideways through the trees and their shadows growing across the trail. Up ahead Miranda stops next to a snow gun. I stop by her side.

"You okay?" I ask.

"Just resting." She wipes her brown cheek with the back of her glove. My eyes flick from her face to the snow gun behind her. The snow gun's stainless steel skin is glistening in the sun. It's mounted on skidders and looks part jet engine, part cannon. Its barrel is pointed skyward, as if aiming to blast soaring eagles out of the sky. Circling the mouth of the barrel is a ring of tiny nozzles where the water comes out and gets blasted into snow. Underneath the gun is a diesel engine that roars when it's making snow. But today it is not making snow. Today the mountain is quiet and the snow gun is pulled off to the side of the trail.

"Your brother" — Miranda takes off her sunglasses and wipes them with her wool gloves — "is crazy if he thinks I'm going to ski that fast."

"Yeah, well, I think he's trying to show Felix something."

"Show Felix what?"

"I don't know." I look away from her. "Maybe by skiing fast he's trying to show Felix that he shouldn't" — I hesitate for a second, as if I have a speech impediment — "say what he said. You know?"

"No. I don't know. I appreciate Bo standing up for me, Sam, but I don't understand how that has anything to do with him skiing so fast."

"Yeah," I mumble, "it probably has nothing to do with him skiing fast." The fact is, I should be skiing fast. How else am I ever going to make it into the top forty?

——————— Sixteen ——————

BO AND I are sitting in the kitchen. We just finished clearing the table and doing the dishes. Now the table is covered with books and notebook paper. I don't mind homework once I'm doing it. It's getting started that's a pain.

There's a quiz tomorrow in geography. There's always a quiz in geography. That way Mrs. Weary doesn't have to teach. It's just as well. She's more boring than all the longitudes and latitudes of this world piled on top of each other. It's not that she's mean, though she has a crooked smile. That's just because her teeth are crooked. Behind her thick glasses her eyes aren't mean. Some teachers have a way of smiling at you while their eyes are cursing you. She's not like that. It's just that when God was dividing out energy and personality He forgot all about her.

It doesn't help that there are only twenty of us in the class. There's no place to hide when she's talking. The worst is when she starts talking about a country's textile production and natural resources. She talks so slowly that her words seem to be coming from the last century. They come out of her mouth covered with hundred-year-old dust.

I pick up my geography book and flip it open to the map of South America. I have to memorize the capitals of every South American country. I start with Colombia and work my way south. I try to stay in South America, but my eyes can't help wandering up through the Caribbean to the Virginia Islands. Last month in English we read Robert Louis Stevenson's *Treasure Island*, and someone told me that the book was set in the Virgin Islands. My finger cruises across the Caribbean like an ocean racer.

"Look." I push the book in front of Bo.

"Hey." He's doing geometry, and spread out all around him is an array of pencils, erasers, rulers, compasses, and a piece of curved plastic with tiny white numbers printed in the shape of a rainbow. He can't believe I covered his stuff with the Caribbean.

"Look." I point to Virgin Gorda. "This is about where Long John Silver buried his treasure."

"Sam, I'm doing parallelograms and trapezoids and you want to talk to me about Long John Silver's treasure."

"I bet you we could find Treasure Island."

"Sam, Treasure Island was fiction. Do you know what fiction means?"

"Yeah."

"It means it never happened. It means Stevenson made it all up."

"Not necessarily."

"What are you talking about?"

"What if Stevenson heard the story from one of Silver's crew members and wrote it down just as it happened?"

"Not very likely."

"But supposing he did? And supposing he told his publishers it was fiction because he wanted them to think he was a clever storyteller and because he didn't want anybody to think that the treasure was real. That way he would be considered a clever writer and he'd be able to find the treasure for himself."

"The only treasure Stevenson found was the book he wrote."

"But suppose there really was a treasure. And suppose Stevenson never found it. We could find it. We could fly down to the Virgin Islands, rent a Boston whaler, and find Treasure Island. It'd be awesome."

"It might be awesome, but I guarantee you there's no treasure. Now, will you let me work?" He shoved the Caribbean across the table at me.

"It'd make an awesome video game, though, wouldn't it? Trying to find Long John Silver's treasure?"

"Sam."

"Yeah." I pull the book back in front of me and stare

at the map. Guiana, Surinam, Guyana, Venezuela. My eyes wander back to the Virgin Islands. But this time they don't stay there. They flip across the page to North America and fly up along the East Coast until they're hovering over western Massachusetts and the Berkshires. We're down there, somewhere, I think. It's just finding us that's hard. I look for the mountains where I'll be racing. I'd need an electron microscope to find them. I flip the book closed and look at Bo. He's mumbling angles and congruencies.

"What do you think the chances are of finding the treasure?"

"Sam." He looks at me hard. "If I flunk this test I'm going to kill you."

"Sorry." I open the book and put my hand over South America. What is the capital of Colombia. Bogotá? I spread my fingers apart. It's Bogotá. Yeah. I feel like I won the lottery. I wonder what the chances are of winning the lottery. Probably about the same as finding Stevenson's treasure; probably about the same as me making the championships.

* ———— **Seventeen** ———— *

"EVERY TIME YOU run a course I want you to picture it in your mind's eye." Phil points down at the bamboo gates. "Do you understand what I'm saying? You have to memorize it. How do you do that? You look at it. You snowplow through it. You study it. And if you have to, you even draw it in the snow." Phil looks down at the course and then takes his pole and stabs holes in the snow symbolizing the first five gates. "Obviously, you don't have to be an artist to do this."

We try not to laugh.

"Why do we do this?" he continues. "We do this first to help us memorize how the gates are positioned and second to help us see the line we want to take through the gates. Who here can tell me what the shortest distance between two points is? Anybody?"

"A straight line," Duncan answers.

"Exactly. But in a race course you have fifty gates, that means fifty points. But the principle is the same. The racer who takes the straightest line through the gates will win." He drags his pole excitedly through the snow. "Do you see? This is the line you have to take. Do you see it?"

He stands there patiently while we study his snow drawing. We're standing at the top of Mountain Meadow, getting an art lesson on the practice course we just set. It's a late Saturday morning and the mountain is already crawling with weekenders in their suburban ski shop outfits. They're the ones in Day-Glo yellow and Day-Glo green one-piece suits. They have two-hundred-dollar ski poles and short skis to maneuver through the chair lift lines.

"Ready to give it a try?" Phil asks.

"Yeah." We nod. We're ready.

"Watch and then follow."

Phil skis halfway through the course, stops, and signals for us to come. Felix goes first, then me.

"Sam," Phil shouts as I pass him. "Stop."

I spray to a stop. He skis down to me.

"That's a real good line, but you keep screwing up your turns. You're turning on both skis and sliding out. Get out over your outside ski, angulate your hip out over that ski." He swings his hip out over his ski. "Do you see, huh? Do see see how my hip is out over that ski? That hip is what's going to power you through your turn and keep you from sliding. Every time your skis slide you lose speed. Every time. You want to keep your speed when you change direction. The only way you can do that is to carve your skis through these turns. *Comprendo?*"

I nod.

"Let's see it."

I get back in the course. I know what Phil's saying. It's getting my body to do it that's hard. My skis scrape through a turn. Did I slide or carve? I don't know. I don't *comprendo.*

———— Eighteen ————

"IT'S YOUR TURN."

"No, it's yours."

"Check the calendar."

"Check it after supper." Mom looks up from her plate.

"Wait a second." I push my chair away from the table. The calendar is taped to the icebox door. For each day of the month there is a square, and scribbled in red pen in the middle of each square is either Bo's name or mine. On the day with our names, we're supposed to wash the dishes. Today is Thursday and my name is scribbled right across the middle of the square.

"But I did them last night. I know I did them last night."

"Last night we had pizza."

"That's not fair. Bo gets out of doing the dishes just because we had pizza."

"You want me to do the dishes at Pizza Hut?"

"Yeah, well, I'm not doing them tonight, then."

"Sam, sit down and finish your supper," Mom scolds.

"Only if I don't have to do the dishes."

"Sam." Mom puts her fork down. Her eyes are squinted almost shut. She looks tired; even her hair looks tired. And there are wrinkles buried in her cheeks that I've never noticed before. "Sam, how many times do you think I've heard that line? It's probably the most used line in all of America, 'I'm not doing the dishes.' "

"Funny."

"I'm not trying to be funny. I'm trying to tell you that if I hear that line just one more time I'll probably have a stroke and die."

"Right."

"And you'll have to pick up the pieces. You'll have to take care of the details of having my body embalmed or cremated or whatever you decide, because I haven't had the time to make plans for such an early death."

"Mom, you're not funny."

"And then you'll have to pick out a casket or an urn. As I think about it, I suppose I'd prefer to be cremated."

"I'll do the dishes."

"You'll have to make arrangements for the service. I'd want flowers, but not so many of them that I would be embarrassed. And then, of course, the details of inviting relatives and guests."

"Bo, will you tell her I'll do the dishes?"

But Bo's just laughing.

"Once I'm dead it will be difficult for me to hold a job. Especially if I've been cremated and there's nothing left of me but a pile of ashes. Can you imagine what it would be like for me to answer the phone or to get dressed? Of course, I wouldn't be able to fit into any of my old clothes. But at least I wouldn't have to worry about dieting anymore. Of course, I wouldn't be able to cook, or do the dishes. I'd probably turn to ink if water got on me."

"Are you through?" I ask.

"That depends."

"I said I'm doing the dishes."

"I suppose I could watch you do the dishes if you kept me in a plastic bag, but it would have to be waterproof and not one that was biodegradable."

"Mom, you are not even funny."

"Can you imagine how awful it would be to have a plastic bag give out in the middle of your son's ski meet?"

"Mom. Bo."

"There I'd be, one minute a self-contained bag of ashes and the next minute nothing but dust in the wind. Isn't that how the *The Treasure of the Sierra Madre* ends?"

"No, that is not how it ends. Stop laughing, Bo. It's gold dust that gets spread in the wind, not some stupid mother's ashes."

"Are you sure?"

"Yes. I'm sure." I turn on the hot water and wring the white plastic bottle of liquid soap into the sink. "And I'm sure of one other thing," I shout over the running water.

"What's that?"

"You left Bo out because you're only mad at me." I throw the dishes into the sink of steaming bubbles.

"Do you want me to tell you about Bo?"

"No, forget it." I turn off the tap and throw my hands into the water. "Just forget it." The soap bubbles crinkle up around my forearms.

——— Nineteen ———

IT'S POURING. The windshield wipers flick back and forth. The headlights disappear into a forest of rain. The pick-up shakes on its chassis as it idles. The inside of the windshield is green from the dashboard lights. The defroster is on full blast and Mom's listening to Nancy Griffith, a skinny country and western singer. She likes her lyrics. I think they're anorexic, but Mom's the driver. So I just sit there and watch the wipers flick against the ice building up along the edges of the windshield. It took us thirty minutes to get here. The roads were sanded, but they were slow and slippery.

"We'll give him another ten minutes," Mom says. "Chances are they've canceled it and we just missed the phone call."

"I don't know, Mom."

"What don't you know?"

"I don't think they cancel races."

"That's ridiculous. Who in their right mind would ski today? Penguins, perhaps?"

"I don't think penguins ski, Mom."

"Sure they do. Haven't you seen that National Geographic special on penguins?"

"No."

"I don't know." She leans forward and tries to look out through the windshield. "I probably should have just turned off the alarm once I heard the rain and gone back to sleep. But no, I drag us out on this God-awful morning, almost drive off the road a couple of times — "

"Here he comes, Mom."

" — nearly killing us just to sit here in this stupid parking lot that they don't have enough sense to pave."

"He's here, Mom."

A set of headlights weaves toward us across the puddles of ice and mud.

"I can't believe it. They really are going to race. I don't know if you should go, Sam."

"It's too late now."

"Damn."

When the rain hits my parka it turns to ice. I stuff my

bag in the back of Phil's van while he's talking to Mom. The van's packed. We do our six o'clock good mornings and I find a space between Josh and Leah. It's a strange fit. Josh is the smallest kid on the team; his parents must be elves or something. Leah is the largest. When God made her He decided He was going to make someone really blond and really big. It's not that she's fat. It's just that's she's as big and round as a beluga, and her skin's almost as white. I can't help thinking she had penguins for breakfast. I try to take off my parka, but it's hard. I'm sitting in her shadow and her shadow weighs a ton. I get my left arm out of its sleeve, then I yank my right arm as hard as I can. Suddenly it jerks free.

"Be still, Sam," she scolds.

"Sorry." I close my eyes and try not to think about Leah or the rain or the race. That's how I skied when I was a little kid. With my eyes half closed, sitting way back on my skis, chewing the thumb of my leather mitten, I was fearless. Felix and I would follow Bo all over the mountain looking for jumps. We'd jump anything that didn't move. We'd jump bumps and moguls, and when there were no bumps or moguls we jumped the shadows of chair-lift towers and trees. When there were no shadows we'd jump nothing but well-groomed snow and we'd turn to each other and say, "See that? How much air did I get?" We'd usually answer, "About a foot," which meant that our skis might have come off the snow. It would be nice if I could race with my eyes closed. Then I wouldn't have to worry about where to make my turns or how steep or icy the course got.

"You guys are going to have to be alert today." Phil pulls out onto Route 2. "It's going to be wet and miserable."

"Is it going to rain all day?" Louie asks.

"You think it'd be wet and miserable if it was going to be sunny?"

"No."

"Isn't it possible to infer from what I am saying, Louie, that it probably will be raining all day?"

"I can't infer."

"And why's that?"

"I don't know what it means."

"Louie," Felix interrupts, "it means it's going to rain all day."

"It's going to rain all day?" Louie asks again.

"If God intends it to, it will rain all day," Josh says in his born-again Christian way. I can't figure out what the born-again means. Josh says it means you get a second chance in everything except racing, which doesn't seem fair to me.

"Chances are it'll rain all day." Phil is in full voice now.

Yeah, we nod, it probably will.

"Anticipating that possibility I have brought a box of garbage bags."

"Garbage bags?" Louie asks. "Why garbage bags?"

"So that you can wear them as ponchos."

As we go around a curve, the back end of the van slips toward the center of the road.

"Geez," Phil mutters as he straightens it out.

"Is it slippery?" Felix asks.

"Is it slippery?" Phil asks. "I remember one time about five years ago we were driving to a race in the freezing rain, just like today. My brother was driving and one of the kids in the back asked him if the road was slippery. My brother whipped open the front door, and with one hand on the steering wheel and the other hand on the door he jumped out of the car and his Sorel boots slid across the macadam like it was ice, which it was. Then he jumped back in the car and asked the kid if that was slippery enough for him."

"Bull," Louie shouts.

"You're lying," Felix adds.

"You think I'm lying?" Phil opens the front door. It roars through the air like a wing. Freezing wind and rain whip at us in the back. We sit straight up. He has one hand on the steering wheel, the other on the open door.

"Daddy!" Molly yells. "Shut that door!"

"You're not lying," Felix shouts.

Phil slams the door shut.

"Never doubt the possible." Phil looks at us in his rearview mirror, his face redder than usual, then drives on as if nothing happened. Molly rolls her eyes up under the top of her eyelids. I lean back in my seat, happy to be in Leah's shadow.

✳——————— **Twenty** ———————✳

IT'S A LONG DAY. Getting to the mountain takes forever. Then there's a long hike through the rain and the ice-covered parking lot. Because we're late there's a long line for registration, a long line for the men's room, a long line for the snack bar. There's a lot of waiting when it's a long day. I lean against a wooden post and close my eyes thinking how I'd rather be lying on the floor of my room reading comics or even memorizing capitals of Central America than standing here.

When we're dressed and ready to go, Phil starts handing out garbage bags. With a pair of scissors he cuts holes at the bottom for our heads, and in the corners he cuts holes for our arms. Molly fits the first bag over her head and it comes down to her boots.

"I like this team look," Felix says when Phil pulls the last bag over his head.

"Yeah, I like it too." Phil puts the scissors back in his ski bag and straightens his hood and goggles. "I just don't want you guys skiing like garbage."

"Dumb. Dumb." We slap him with our gloves.

"Boy, you guys have no sense of humor." He pushes through the double doors and we follow him into the pouring rain. He doesn't make us hike the course. In our green plastic shells, we ride the chair lift doubled over like turtles, trying to do the impossible of staying dry. We slide quickly through the course and race back to the lodge, where we stand dripping under a covered porch.

"The course is a freeway." Phil wipes the half-frozen

rain off his goggles. "Just straight ahead. They want to get the race over fast. When I take the girls up, you guys stay inside. When they come in everybody but Sam come up. Sam, when the guys come in, you come up. This way everyone won't be standing around in the rain."

When Phil, Molly, and Leah step out into the rain, the rest of us go inside. We play videos and sit at a table in the corner of the lodge watching the rain freeze on the plate glass windows. It's so dark outside that it looks like night. Leah and Molly come in dripping wet and the guys leave. Time is weird. Whenever I look up at the clock, the second hand hasn't moved. But then suddenly the guys are hanging over the table like rain clouds and I'm riding up the chair lift in the freezing rain. Then I'm in the starting gate, the starter is counting down, and I'm trying to look through the film of ice and water covering my goggles. When he says go, I ski through a world of water. Occasionally I see a blue or red gate, and when I finally get to the bottom I don't wait around to hear my time. They don't stop to reset the course for the second run. They don't even stop for lunch. When I come stumbling into the lodge, Molly and Leah have already gone to the top. It's only a matter of time before I'm back out there racing through the rain with my eyes half closed. And then we're in the van riding home. Everyone is wet, but no one is complaining. Phil's driving with one hand. With the other hand he's holding the results. He looks from the windshield to the results, from the results to the windshield. We're not happy about the way he's driving, but at least the roads aren't slippery anymore and he hasn't opened the front door.

"Not bad." He turns around and looks at us. We all

cringe. Duncan reaches over and puts a hand on the steering wheel. Phil nudges Duncan's hand away and turns halfway around so that one eye is on the road, the other on us. "You know, when people look at my kids and say, 'Phil's kids are gutsy. They aren't bothered by a little freezing rain,' I'm really proud. You kids were gutsy today. I don't care if you finished or fell, you all had gutsy runs. And Sam, is it possible you crept up another five places in the rain? You're sure making those kids ahead of you nervous."

"It's still a long way from the top forty," I mumble.

"The top forty?" In the rearview mirror I see Phil raise his eyebrows. "Who's talking about the top forty?"

"Yeah." Louie slaps me on the head with his wet hat.

I turn around and stare at him. For the first time since I've known him, I realize he has fat lips. And suddenly I'm overcome by this urge to slug him right in the middle of his fat-lipped grin, if only he were smaller.

* ——— **Twenty-one** ——— *

I DON'T GET IT. I sit on the floor of my room, surrounded by plastic pieces wrapped in vacuum-packed plastic bags. The top of the box is balanced on my knees. I study the picture of the radio car on the cover. I go from the picture to the plastic packets, trying to find the shock absorbers. The packets have white labels with an eight-number code printed on them. Nothing as simple as a label in English that says "Shock absorber." It's as if they want to make you a hostage to the directions.

"I don't get it," I mutter.

"Huh?" Bo mumbles without looking up. He's lying on my bed, reading comics.

"I don't get it."

"What?" He drops the comic book, rolls onto his side, and looks over the edge of the bed. "What are you doing?"

"Building a radio car."

"Doesn't look like a radio car."

"Will you shut up?"

"Well, I don't get it. If you want a radio car, why don't you buy one already made?"

"Because it's more fun to make it."

"Oh, I get it, and the complaining is just part of the fun you're having."

"Will you shut up? I'm not complaining. I just can't figure out which pieces are in which bags."

"Read the directions."

"It's more fun to do it without reading the directions."

"Okay, if you're not going to listen to my advice, why interrupt me?"

"Interrupt you? You're reading comics. You can't interrupt someone who's reading comics."

"Yeah, well, you can't build a radio car without reading the directions."

"The directions are translated from Japanese. They don't make any sense."

"Building a radio car without directions is like trying to race without coaching."

"Who's talking about racing? I'm building a car. I'm not getting ready for some race. I just finished a race. I don't want to talk about racing."

"Why are you so touchy?"

"Because I'm okay at building radio cars, but I suck at racing."

"Who said you suck at racing?"

"Me."

"Yeah, well, I hate to disappoint you, but looking at the mess you're making I'd say you're a better racer."

"That's why Phil is always telling me what I'm doing wrong? That's why he keeps telling me to forget about making the top forty?"

"He's telling you what you're doing wrong to make you a better racer. And he's probably telling you not to think about the top forty to keep you from getting tense."

"Yeah, right." I rip open the side of the box, grab the directions, and nearly tear them in half as I try to unfold them.

"And start at the beginning." He rolls back into the middle of my bed and picks up his comic book.

"Oh, yeah?" My eyes flick down to the last panel of directions and come to rest on number fifty-six.

"Yeah. When you learn to race, it's the cumulative details of racing technique that make you ski fast. It's the cumulative details of the directions that . . ."

I stop listening. I can't help it. Something inside my brain just flicks off. When people who think they're right start talking I get claustrophobic. It's as if their rightness vaporizes any possibilities or choices. The space around me shrinks while their rightness grows unchecked. Everything about them becomes right. When they talk their tone of voice is right, their teeth and lips are right, their posture is right, their eyes and hair glow with rightness. I can just tell that Bo is glowing with rightness behind that comic.

Somehow my eyes find number one of the instructions, and in italics the heading reads *Getting Started: Building Your Car's Shock Absorbers.*

What I hate most about people who think they're right, is when they're right.

———— Twenty-two ————

SOMETIMES SCHOOL DRAGS. Sometimes it flies. Today algebra is over before I know it. Felix and I were both at the board most of the period. He was doing a problem from last night's set. I was doing a "just suppose" problem that Mr. Reilly pulled out of thin air. It was a struggle to grasp, especially with all of Felix's interruptions. It never occurs to Felix that I might have to think to answer his questions. He just assumes that the answers are like loose change in my pocket. All I have to do is reach in and pull out whatever he needs. It's hard enough doing one of Mr. Reilly's "just suppose" problems without having to do Felix's work while pretending I'm just doing my own.

Geography goes even faster than algebra. Mrs. Weary gives us a test on the countries of Central America. It doesn't take me long, so I spend extra time shading in each country with a different colored pencil. When I hand it in, Mrs. Weary is sitting at her desk, her head resting in her hands. She yawns, takes the map, and puts on her glasses.

"Do you want me . . ." She yawns again and puts a hand to her mouth. "Excuse me, do you want me to grade this now or later?"

"Doesn't matter."

"I'll do it later, then. You can go back to your seat or you can be excused and go to the library."

I go to the library. Not that I like being there. Our librarian is an anti-librarian. She sprays her black hair into a helmet and she wears the same expression of exasperation on her face day after day. Whenever I walk into the library she looks at me the way a cop looks when he pulls a car over for speeding. I walk on my toes when I'm in there. In the fall she yelled at me every time she saw me because, she said, I hadn't returned a book I had returned weeks earlier. In the middle of a math exam she stormed into the room and started yelling at me that I couldn't take the exam because I hadn't returned the book. Mr. Reilly asked her to leave. Later, in the hall, she threatened to have me expelled. Then she found the book on her desk.

"Can you imagine that? I must have misplaced it."

"No, I can't imagine that."

I never expected an apology. Adults who don't like kids don't understand that the rules for kids are the same as the rules for adults. It doesn't occur to them that we have feelings, that we breathe and eat and sleep just the way they do. It's almost like they think we're from another planet, or that we're not even alive.

"Next time you may not be so lucky."

"Next time you misplace a book, don't blame me."

"Young man, don't be impertinent!" She glared angrily at me over her half glasses. Phil would probably say her glasses have been cut in half because that's all she can see of the world. A whole pair of glasses would just be a waste of correction.

Thinking about this I decide to skip the library and go to the cafeteria instead. The whole tenth grade is there for study hall, but they're not studying. Most of the guys are shooting rubber bands at the girls and the girls are shaking their heads disapprovingly and shooting rubber bands at the guys. I sit down at an empty table, pick up yesterday's paper, and flip through the sports section until the bell rings. Then I go to English.

English is different. Our teacher, Mrs. Blake, is from England, and she's as English and as regal as the queen, and just as proper. It's not that she has us diagramming sentences all day, it's just that she doesn't let us get away with anything.

"We will not tolerate half-baked thoughts," she told Felix's class at the beginning of the year.

"How about microwaved?" Felix asked her.

"I beg your pardon?"

"How about if the thoughts are microwaved?"

Felix spent the rest of the period standing in the hall. Word got around fast: Don't give her lip.

We sit in our seats quietly, our *Tales of the Greek Heroes* opened to the chapter on Hercules. When the door flies open we all stand. She's the only teacher we do this for. She strides in smiling and nodding at us, her coat thrown over her shoulders like a cape. She drapes the coat over the desk, takes out her copy of our book, and sits down on top of her coat. Her gray hair is white in the late-afternoon sun, shining on her like a spotlight.

"I apologize for being late. Now, class, where were we?"

"Hercules' choice," Lillia, who dyed her hair red last night, answers.

"Yes, and has everyone read today's assignment?" Not stopping to hear our answers, she begins to read the passage out loud. I close my eyes. Her voice is full of theatrical accents, and listening to her is almost like watching a movie.

Hercules is in a high mountain meadow, tending cows, wondering, Is this all there is to life? when out of nowhere two beautiful women come walking across the meadow toward him. The first is dressed in white, her hair is drawn back modestly, and her eyes are natural. She is Virtue. The second is wearing beautifully colored clothes, her hair is done up with ornamental combs, and her face is painted to accentuate her beauty. She wears jewelry and walks like a woman who enjoys being admired. She strides up to Hercules.

"Come with me," she urges. "With me life will be easy and pleasurable. You shall taste every pleasure."

"What is your name?"

"Hercules, those who love me call me Happiness."

Then the first woman speaks. "I too have come to offer you a way of life. Follow me and you will do great deeds, but you cannot win what is glorious and excellent in this world without care and hard work."

When Mrs. Blake finishes reading, she looks up from

her book and smiles. "Well, class, besides stating the obvious, what have you to say about this passage?"

No one says anything.

"Perhaps I should rephrase that question. What have you to say about this passage and, please, do state the obvious."

Our hands shoot up in the air.

"Yes, William."

William wears his hair parted in the middle and slicked back. His clothes look as if he stole them from a fifty-year-old man. In fact, William acts like a fifty-year-old man. He talks slowly, as if the thoughts he's thinking are so powerful that they'd blow his teeth out of his mouth if he let them come out too fast.

"Hercules" — he clears his throat — "liked the" — he stares around the room to give the words a chance to clear his teeth — "simpler things" — he coughs into his hand — "of life."

"What do you mean by that, William?"

"Just that." His eyes wander again. "He liked the woman" — he swallows hard. I want to slap him on the back to get the rest of the sentence out, but I don't. I just grind my teeth — "in the plain dress" — he swallows more air — "better than the woman in the fancy dress." He finishes in a kind of rush. His face is all red. He puts his hand to his mouth to make sure he hasn't blown any of his teeth out.

"Yes, that's correct as far as it goes. Anybody else?"

William wants to say more, but he's exhausted from his efforts. Lillia puts up her hand.

"Yes, Lillia."

"I feel that Hercules is making a choice that all of us will have to make at some point in our lives."

"And what is that, dear?"

"Whether we're going to party all our lives or work hard."

"Very good. Do you think Hercules would have been famous if he had chosen Vice instead of Virtue? Darkness instead of light?"

"No." Everybody shakes their heads.

"You don't seem to agree, Sam."

"What?" I look up at her. Across the room in the late-afternoon light she looks like she's dressed in white.

"Do you think Hercules would have been famous had he chosen Vice instead of Virtue?"

"Possibly." I blink at her through the light, thinking this reminds me of something. What does it remind me of?

"And do you want to tell us your reasons?"

"Well." I look around the room. William is staring straight at me, a stupid fifty-year-old grin on his face. "I sort of feel that Hercules was bound to be famous. It was in his genes. I mean, after all, he was Zeus's son. If he had gone with Vice he probably would be remembered as the world's number-one party animal."

"But," she allows herself a slight smile, "he didn't choose to take that path."

"No, ma'am, he took Virtue seriously."

"And what does that mean, Sam?"

"I guess it means he realized, you know" — I scan my memory for the right words — "that if he wanted a life beyond the glitter of beauty and pleasure, he had to work hard. You know? He had to really care and be virtuous to do what he wanted."

"And what did he want to do?"

"I don't know. Great deeds?"

"Exactly — " The bell interrupts, but no one moves. We sit there with our books open.

"That was well done, class. I would say that many of you have a Herculean understanding of this." She smiles to herself as if she's just made a joke and then adds, "Pages 128–149. Class dismissed."

——— Twenty-three ———

I LIE IN BED half asleep, listening to Sting. Here and there on the ceiling are fragments of moonlight that are somehow reflected from the windows. The best thing about lying in bed is that it's the one place where a kid doesn't have to do all the dumb things he's supposed to do. I lie there half dreaming, half remembering my last lesson with Mary. Bo and Felix are there and we're climbing up the side of the beginner's slope, when my skis split apart and I fall between them. I keep my face out of the snow by holding myself up with my elbows.

"Come on, Sam, don't you want to get on the J bar?" Felix and Bo call.

"Yeah," I mumble as I try to pull my skis together. "I want to go up the J bar." The J bar is like a lot of things in life. If you know anything about it before you do it, you might never do it, but I didn't know anything about it. When I climb up the side of the beginner's slope, I see the J-bar house for the first time. It looked just the way it does today, small and white with a green roof. Behind it is a tower with a huge pulley pulling a cable of dangling J bars down the hill. The lines for the J bar are roped off and skiers are holding their poles in one hand and with their other are holding on to the rope and pulling themselves along. Bo and Felix and Mary move ahead with the line, but every time I let go of the rope to grab farther ahead I slip backward. There are other skiers around me, and when I fall through the ropes I study their boots and bindings. Mary comes back for me, untangles me from the rope, lifts me up by the armpits, and carries me to the front of the line.

"Keep your skis together, Sam," Mary instructs as she skates out to the attendant and puts me down.

"Two for the price of one." The attendant smiles.

"More like ten for the price of one," Mary answers without smiling.

The attendant places the bottom of the J bar behind Mary and steps away. Nothing happens. Then suddenly we start gliding up the slope. Mary holds a gloved hand over my chest, her knees pressed tight against my rib cage, her skis on both sides of mine.

"Keep your skis in the tracks," she instructs.

I chew on the end of my frozen mitten, concentrating on keeping my skis in the track. Halfway up I lose my concentration and one of my skis wanders over on top of Mary's. She starts sliding to the right, I start sliding to the left. Somehow she keeps our balance.

"Geez, Mary," I mumble as we come back together, "you want to kill me."

"Geez, Sam," she mumbles back, "the thought never crossed my mind."

Bo and Felix are waiting for us at the top, smiling, pointing, talking so fast I can't understand them. We slide over to them and Mary begins our lesson.

"Snowplowing is how you stop, and from it you will learn how to turn. First, I want you to make a V with your skis so that the tips are pointed at each other. That's right, Bo. That's right, Felix. No, Sam, don't cross your skis. That's an X."

"An X?" I try to remember what a V looks like.

"An X will make you fall."

"An X will make me fall?"

"Sam, do you know what a V looks like?"

"I know the alphabet. *A, b, c, d, e, f, g . . .*"

"That's good, Sam."

"*H, i, j, k.*"

"Sam, why don't you just follow me. Look at what I'm doing and try to do the same thing. Felix and Bo, you follow Sam."

"But what comes after *k?*" I ask.

She starts down the slope. "Follow me and I'll tell you, okay?"

"Okay." I start after her.

"*L,*" she says and turns to her left.

"*L,*" I say and go straight down the mountain.

I don't think to yell. I just stick out my tongue, squint hard through my goggles, and try not to fall. Other beginner skiers sort of shuffle out of my way. When I get to the bottom I feel a warm tingling all over. I look down at my pants to see if they're wet. They aren't. So, this is skiing.

"Way to go, Sam." Felix races up to me. "You were flying."

"Yeah." I smile. "I was flying."

It was like a miracle. I had done something I barely dared dream possible. In the short space of holding my breath, I had gone from constantly falling down and lying with my face in the snow to flying out of control down the beginner's slope.

The tape ends and I lie there for a minute, listening to the silence, smiling at the memory. Then I pop out the cassette and grab another tape off the bureau. I try to read the label in the moonlight, but I can't. I stick it in, readjust the earphones, and press Play. Guitar then trumpet. Reggae bass and drum. Then Jimmy Cliff singing, "You can get it if you really want. . . . But you must try, try, and try."

When the song ends I'm sitting straight up, sweating. A feeling, like a memory, is glowing somewhere in my stomach. I've listened to this song a thousand times, but I've never heard those words before. I press Rewind. The sweating stops, but the feeling lingers. "Got your mind set on a dream. . . . You can get it the harder it seems. . . . You can get it if you really want it." It never occurred to me before that that was possible. I just thought things happened or didn't happen, that dreams come true or don't come true of their own accord. It never occurred to me that if I want something I can get it if I try. It never occurred to me that that's what might have happened to me on the beginner's slope, that that's what might be happening to me now. I play the tape over and over. And when I fall asleep I can't tell if the glow on the ceiling is moonlight, memory, or me.

—————— Twenty-four ——————

JANUARY IS THE MONTH of darkness. We wake up in the dark. We go to school in the dark. While we're in class the sun comes out, but by the time we get home it's dark again. February is the month of coming light. Now when we wait for the bus, the sun is beginning to rise, and when we get home the sun is only just setting.

We stand in front of the race shack waiting for Phil. It's eight-thirty in the morning, but already the sun is warm on our backs. We're cold, but we're not freezing to death. We can actually talk and move our arms and legs. I don't know who throws the first snowball. All I know is that one minute we're standing there, talking, yawning, and stretching, and the next minute we're hiding behind the pines whipping snowballs through the air.

When Phil steps out the door of the race shack it isn't that he accidentally walks into one of our snowballs. It's more that the snowballs turn in midair and come whistling at him. The rest of the snowballs come whipping out of our hands, nailing him to the door. At first he doesn't do much. He just leans against the door, puts an arm over his head, and kind of ducks underneath it. But when that doesn't stop the snowballs from coming, he grabs a breakaway gate and charges us. Attacking the snowballs like a karate master, he swings the pole with a jerky motion, shattering the snowballs into powder. He kicks. He grunts. When he shrieks we run.

One hundred sit-ups, one hundred pushups, on a cold blanket of snow. Then we hike up the mountain carrying our skis and bamboo poles on our shoulders. Phil says nothing. But every twenty yards he stops, drills a hole, puts out his hand for a pole, and jams it into the snow. You can't tell with Phil whether he's faking being mad or he's really mad. You just can't tell. By the time we get halfway up the Eastern Trail, we're all sweating, our parkas are unzipped, and our hats are in our pockets. Phil sets the last pole and straightens up.

"Okay, guys, listen up." He wipes his forehead with the back of his glove. "Tomorrow's our last race before the championships. The race is going to be right here on Eastern. There are going to be two runs of GS. Does everyone understand that?"

We nod.

"Good. Now we've had our little snowball fight. We've had our pushups and sit-ups. We've had our little hike up the mountain. I'd like to think that now we're ready to do some serious training. What I want is ten good runs this morning, ten quality runs, and then no practice this afternoon."

"Yeah!" we all cheer.

"Now, I'm not letting you out early so you can hang out at the mall. I want you to get your skis done before supper and I want you in bed before nine. You understand?"

We nod.

"Tomorrow's a big day. How some of you do tomorrow is going to determine where you start in the championships. By Tuesday I'll know the results, so let's meet here after school, okay?" He doesn't wait for us to answer. "Now, I want you to ski each run this morning like a race. I want race-type concentration. I don't want you thinking about lunch or videos. I want you thinking about skiing. I want you to find the rhythm of the course and I want you to get into it. I want you to think about going fast and I want you to think about being technically correct. Do you understand? Leah, you're first."

Leah clicks into her skis, slides to the starting gate, and takes off.

"Guys," Phil shouts, "I want you to explode out of your start. I want you to attack the course. I don't want you skiing it like Sunday drivers. Molly, you're next. I want you to attack it from the start."

Molly double-poles out of the starting gate and skates to the first turn.

"Angulate," Phil yells after her. He turns to us. "Guys, you have to get out over that outside ski. You can't just bend your knee so your ski is on edge. You have to drive those hips out over the ski so it carves through the turn. You understand? Duncan."

I watch each of the guys go until Phil and I are the only ones left at the top of the course. I snowplow into the starting gate, trying to remember Phil's list of instructions.

"Sam." Phil stands in front of me. He puts his gloved hands on my shoulders and looks me right in the eye. It's hard to look Phil in the eyes. Even through his goggles his eyes are blue flames. I look at his mouth. He says, "I've been thinking about what you said, about wanting to get in the top forty. I don't want you to think that I was discouraging you. I just don't want you pressuring yourself. The truth is you're right on the edge of putting it all together. I don't know when it'll happen, but when it does you'll definitely have a shot at the top forty. Now, let's make this run technically the best run of your life. Feel the rhythm of the mountain."

*——— **Twenty-five** ———*

I KEEP WAKING with the sheets tied around me in knots. Phil is standing on my bureau, the size of a trophy, talking to me in a high metallic voice.

"You're going to do it, Sam. You're going to break into the top forty and you're going to make the championships." Then he tells me in detail how I'm going to do it. Part of me understands what he's saying. Part of me tingles like a foot that's fallen asleep. I try hard to understand him. I can see the words coming out of his mouth, completely spelled out. It's just that for some reason I can't read them. It's as if they're in a foreign language.

When I look up at the bureau he's gone. I unravel the wet sheets, smooth them out with my feet. My pillow feels as if it's filled with rocks. I shake it and the rocks break into clumps of foam. I don't even know if I want to make the championships. I don't even know if I want to try. I look at the clock. It's only twelve-thirty.

The next time I wake I'm freezing. My blankets and sheets are gone. My pillow is gone. I grope around the bed in the dark. I can't find anything. I reach down to the floor. A wool hand grabs at me. I snap back in bed, turn on the light — nothing on the floor but my blankets and sheet. I pull them back onto the bed and turn off the light. I look at the clock. It's 4:00 A.M. I wrap the covers around me and try to find that soft comfortable spot that has nothing to do with the bed, but only to do with me. I don't know what time it is when I find it. But I know I found it because I dream.

I'm racing down a white mountain feeling the logic of rhythm. It's as if the rhythm has eyes that tell me when to turn, when to roll my hips, when to transfer my weight. The tips and tails of my skis feel as natural as the toes and heels of my feet. Run after run, I carve smoothly between the red and blue gates. It's like dancing, and I can almost hear the music.

I wake up to a song. Bo is standing in my door. That's when I realize it's not the words that are important. It's the rhythm. The feeling.

Twenty-six

IT'S NOT THAT I'm nervous. It's just that I don't hear Mom talking to me. I mean I hear her. It's just the first time through I don't get what she's saying. She's pretty patient. She asks two or three times before I get the meaning.

"Do you want fried or scrambled eggs?" I finally hear.

"Scrambled," I answer. I don't know why I say scrambled. I'd rather have fried. But scrambled is what comes out.

I don't do much better with Bo. He's sitting across from me eating his eggs and talking at me. I don't know what he's saying. I don't touch the eggs. I concentrate on the words coming out of his mouth. Slowly, I begin to get it, but I don't know if I'm hearing the words or reading his lips.

"What's wrong with you?"

"Nothing," I hear myself answer.

"Well, will you stop staring at me? You're giving me the creeps."

"What did you say?"

"I said, Will you stop staring at me."

"I mean before that."

"Before what?"

"Before you said, Stop staring at me."

"I was talking to you about today's race, but you're so far in the ozone you didn't hear a thing."

"What did you say?"

"You're nervous."

"I am not nervous."

"Right."

"Why should I be nervous?"

"Because you care how you do."

"I don't care how I do."

"Right, like it's not okay to care." Bo calls into the kitchen, "Mom, isn't it okay to care how you do?"

"Of course." Mom walks into the room carrying a cup of coffee. I watch the steam spiral up past her chin and green eyes.

"See? And if you care how you do, you're going to be nervous, right, Mom?"

"Right." She sits down next to me and puts a long slender hand on my shoulder. "Eat your eggs and listen to what Bo's telling you."

I pick up my fork and start eating. The eggs are between being warm and okay and being cold and rubbery.

"All I was saying is it's okay to be nervous, and if you know that, you can use your nervousness."

"What are you talking about?" I rip a piece of toast in half.

"Nervousness can be like extra energy to help you ski at a higher level. You understand?"

Yeah, I nod, even though I don't have a clue to what he's saying. I start eating my eggs. Mom and Bo keep talking about nerves and performance. I look at the box of Wheaties, wishing I could slam dunk.

———— Twenty-seven ————

WE WATCH LEAH and Molly. Then we take off our skis and scrape them. We're at the top of Eastern. The start is a hundred yards below us. Every now and then I look out over the snow-covered corn fields and the ice-covered river thousands of feet below. Up here there's nothing but mountaintops and blue sky.

"Boys' starting order." A fat man with a raspy voice and a faded tan parka shouts out numbers one through fifteen.

I look down at the bib on my chest. I'm ninety-three, still way back in the pack. Upside-down it reads thirty-six. I wish I were thirty-sixth. I step into my bindings, pull on my gloves, and tighten the Velcro straps around the wrists. I grab my poles and snowplow down to the start. When I get there, Felix and Duncan are already stripped down to their GS suits, Felix in the blue-black, Duncan in silver. I snap out of my skis and slide down on my boots to the second gate.

The first kid is Durell. He's already in the starting gate. He shakes his head and shoulders, puts his poles over the wand, and starts. Usually I watch the kids' faces, but today for some reason I watch their skis all the way down the steeps. Sometimes they're late, sometimes they slide, but mostly they're fast. They all ski it about the same way. When it's Felix's turn I shout, click my poles, and try to whistle between my lower teeth. He looks good, as if he's on the U.S. ski team in his dark, blue suit. I forget to watch Duncan. I mean I watch him;

I just forget it's him. But I cheer for Josh and Louie and then I climb up to get ready for my turn. To stay warm I run up Eastern. It's so steep it's more like climbing than running, and I have to kick my toes into the hard snow to keep from falling. By the time I get to the top, sweat's pouring off my face and I'm out of breath. I turn around and ski down on the soles of my boots. I hit a patch of ice and nearly fall as I dance over it. The rest of the way I barely keep my balance, I'm going so fast.

"Sam." Phil waves me over to him. "Ten minutes to crank it up."

I unzip my warm-ups and step out of them, take off my parka, and pull the bib down over my red slalom sweater. I grab the back ties, wrap them around the front, and tie them. Phil takes the front ties, pulls them around my back, and knots them. The whole time he's talking to me.

"This is your mountain, Sam. This mountain knows who you are. It knows how you ski. It knows all your rhythms. It's not going to let you blow a single turn."

I nod and pull my goggles over my eyes. Then I step into my bindings so that the racing edges are inside. I loop my gloves through the leather straps of my poles.

"Ninety-three," a voice calls.

"That's us, Sam."

We glide over to the start.

"Just remember this is your mountain. You know its moods and rhythms. This mountain belongs to you, Sam. Don't let anybody take it away from you."

"Yeah." His eyes could be stars.

"You got to want it."

"Yeah." My lips and mouth are suddenly dying-of-thirst dry. I look down the course and curve my right hand through the first gates as though it were me. Back and forth. Back and forth. Trying to feel the rhythm.

"Get yourself ready, ninety-three."

I take a deep breath, click my poles together, and carefully put them over the starting wand.

"Five, four, three — "

"It's your mountain, kid." Phil is right behind me.

" — two, one, go!"

"Go, Sam, go."

I want to say I'm going, I'm going, but before I can, I'm gone.

* —————— **Twenty-eight** —————— *

I RACE UPSTAIRS to the second floor of the lodge. It's packed with racers. Some of them have the tops of their GS suits unzipped and tied around their waists. Others are in street clothes. They're all eating, drinking, and talking. I squeeze down an aisle and step over ski boots, duffel bags, and lunch coolers to where the guys are sitting. I pull off my hat and goggles as I walk. There's so much body heat.

"Sam," Felix calls, "how'd you do?"

"Not so good." I sit down next to him. "I didn't wait around to find out. How'd you do?"

He holds up five fingers.

"Yeah." I reach over and slap his hand, palms up.

"What about you, Duncan?"

He holds up eight fingers. Felix beat him? I try not to show my surprise as I slap his hand.

I look at Josh, but before I can ask he holds his thumb upside-down.

"You biffed?" I ask.

"Yeah." He shrugs his shoulders.

"Bummer."

I don't ask Louie how he did, even though he's sitting there staring at me with his fat-lipped grin. Instead I ask, "Where are Leah and Molly?"

"They've already gone out to check the course for the second run," Duncan says. "You better eat because we got to get out there too."

By the time I finish my peanut butter and jelly sandwich, the room is emptying out. Felix gets up and gives me a shove.

"Come on, Sam. We are forever waiting for you. You got to get yourself in the top forty so you can hang with us."

"Fat chance." Louie laughs as he shoves past me.

I finish my juice and throw the empty box in a trash can. I wipe peanut butter off the sides of my mouth as I follow the guys downstairs.

Outside it's warm in the sun. We click into our skis and glide over to the chair lift, our goggles down around our necks, our hats in our pockets. At the top of the mountain we cut over to Eastern and snow-plow down to the start. The sun on the snow is so bright we have to put on our goggles. Phil is nowhere around so Duncan and Felix start taking us through the course.

"Straight, straight," Duncan and Felix call over their shoulders as they snowplow through the first eight gates. The rest of us are snowplowing right behind them.

"Whoa." Felix and Duncan stop at the ninth gate and the three of us pull up next to them.

"Geez." Duncan looks at the gate way over to our left. "And how the hell are we supposed to get over there?"

"Who set this course?" Felix shakes his head. "Straight as an express and then this red cranker. We're going to have so much speed when we hit this sucker, there are going to be more than a few blowouts here."

Duncan points to the gate just above us. "As we go through that blue, we got to start our turn for this red or we'll never make it."

"Yeah." Felix looks up the course. "You guys see that?"

We're all staring up at the blue gate when Molly, Leah, and Phil spray to a stop next to us.

"Who the hell set this course and how the hell are we supposed to make this turn?" Felix holds the palms of his gloves up in the air, his poles dangling from his wrists.

Phil smiles. "Well, I'll tell you one thing. You're not going to make this turn if you're not aggressive. If you guys don't go out and attack it, if you don't get out on that downhill ski, forget it. It's over. You guys inspect the whole course yet?"

We shake our heads.

"What have you been doing?"

"Playing videos," Felix lies. "You should have seen my score."

"Terrific." Phil knows he's lying. He looks at his watch. "Only fifteen minutes before the girls' run. Leah and Molly, hike up to the start and get ready. You guys better finish checking out the course. I don't want to see your faces for another twenty minutes."

"You don't like my face?" Felix's teeth sparkle in the sun as he tries not to smile.

Phil looks at Felix, then at the rest of us, a half smile on his face. His eyes are asking us if we can believe this kid.

"Just check out the course, will you?"

"Yeah." Felix starts gliding away from us.

"And Felix."

"What?" He stops and looks over his shoulder.

"I like your face."

"Thanks." He shakes his head and takes off. We start after him.

"Sam," Phil calls.

I jam my skis around, stop, and look up the hill.

"Not a bad first run." His smile is like Felix's. All teeth.

"It was okay."

"You okayed yourself right into forty-third place. I'd call that slightly better than okay."

"You're lying."

"I'm not lying."

"You sure it was me?"

"You're the only ninety-three on the mountain."

"I got forty-third?"

"You got forty-third, and do you know what that means?"

"Yeah."

"It means you're starting forty-third on the second run. So don't go hanging out with those guys in the back of the pack."

"I won't."

"And Sam" — he takes off his right glove and holds his thumb and forefinger a hair apart — "you're only this far from the top forty."

———— Twenty-nine ————

I WAIT AT the top of Eastern. I'm not cold but my legs are shaking. I'm not nervous, I tell myself. I try to remember what Bo said. What did he say about being nervous? Why am I so nervous? I wasn't this nervous in the morning and nothing's changed. It's the same race. It's the same mountain. It's the same sky. Get a hold of yourself, kid — that's what Bo would say. How am I going to get a hold of myself? I take a deep breath and look down the mountain. My arms and back are shivering. I look down the course. I watch Duncan, then Felix. They both smoke through the upper part of the course. Duncan takes the blue gate wide so that he has plenty of space to come across to the red cranker. Felix takes it tight, right on the gate, and almost falls. Should

I take it wide or tight? I step into my bindings. With my legs still shaking, I snowplow down to the start. I'm going to take it wide.

"Louie, get your skis on. Sam, warm up." Phil points back up the Eastern. I click out of my bindings and start running. Little sparks of ice fly out where my toes kick the snow. At each step my breath pounds out of me. My legs burn, but I don't stop. I want to run over the top of the mountain into the state forest and leave this race behind. I finally stop halfway to the top, turn, and slide back down. By the time I get back, Louie's gone and Phil's clapping his gloves.

"Come on, Sam."

I clean the bottom of my boots and click into my bindings. I adjust my goggles, put my gloves through the straps of my poles, and glide over to Phil, who's standing in line.

"A little tense?"

I nod. He rubs my arms and shoulders. I take a deep breath. My lungs half open, hesitate, and then like the fingers of a fist, open all the way. Phil's voice is somewhere inside my brain.

"This is your mountain, Sam. This morning sure proved that. And this is your day. It's coming together for you. You're right on the edge, old buddy. It's your day and your mountain, so just let those skis run. Find the rhythm, and the mountain will take care of the rest."

"Ninety-three," the starter calls out. "Come get yourself set, please."

"That's us, Sam."

I glide into the start and stare down at the course. My right hand curves through the gates trying to find that rhythm. I put my poles over the starting wand.

The starter counts down. "Five, four, three, two . . ."

I kick my heels in the air and I'm gone.

The top is fast and straight. I'm not worried about these turns. I'm worried about the cranker. Wide or tight? What did I decide? I whip tight past the blue gate and into the cranker. I'm tight. I jam the turn. I try to stay out over my downhill ski, but the force of the turn drives me back into the mountain.

Snow and ice splatter everywhere.

"This is your mountain."

My skis fly sideways, chattering across the hard snow, and then somehow catch and catapult me through the red gate. I land off balance.

"You're right on the edge, old buddy."

The next gate is rushing straight at me. Somehow I get my weight over both skis as I slice through the gate. By the next gate I'm under control.

"Today's your day."

I come over the knoll and down the final stretch. The rhythm of the gates is in my legs. An icicle of sweat is dripping down my spine. I don't breathe until I cross the finish line. I ski out of the finish area. Under the pine trees I double over, gasping for air.

Someone is pounding me on the back. I look up and Felix's face is upside-down. "You idiot." He smiles. "That run just put you in thirty-sixth place."

Thirty

WAITING IS LIKE dying. There's no end to it. It takes forever for Tuesday to come. That's a long time for a kid. It's like being buried alive. Just getting through Sunday night is a miracle. My blood is like warm soda. Homework is like Sanskrit. I just stare at it, and when I can't stare at it anymore I do chin-ups on the bar in my closet and sit-ups on the floor. I go looking for Bo to play cards with, but he's doing his homework. I walk ten miles through the house. I eat four bowls of cereal, listen to endless tapes. That night I dream that I sleep with my eyes open. In the morning I wake up exhausted. I eat breakfast and go back to bed. I wake up at eleven and sit in a chair in the living room watching dust motes whirling through sunlight like Phil's words.

"Did he make it?" someone had asked.

"Sure looks like it, but we'll have to wait and see," Phil answered.

Later I fall asleep at the supper table. Mom takes my temperature. It's normal, but she still makes me go to bed. All night I keep dreaming about my second run. At the red cranker my skis go out from underneath me. I hit the snow hard on my back. With the wind knocked out of me I bounce into the air, my arms sprawling, my legs crossed. When I land there's a sickening sound of something breaking. I wake up with my legs bathed in sweat.

——— Thirty-one ———

WE SIT IN FRONT of the race shack, waiting for Phil. It's warm in the sun. I can smell the sap from the wood siding and the pines. I have to squint when I look up the slope, sunlight reflecting off the white snow. We talk a little, mostly about nothing. We say nothing about the championships. We say nothing about what we're waiting for. Mostly we just wait, listening for Phil's van. When we finally hear it coming around the corner, I suddenly wish Tuesday wasn't until tomorrow.

He stands in front of us, his back to the sun, his face in shadow. He's wearing his Boston Red Sox hat, blue jeans that just touch the tops of his work boots, a shirt and tie under a down vest.

"Settle down, guys."

The guys stop punching each other and the girls stop giggling. He takes a piece of paper out of his vest pocket as if he has to read what he's about to say. He glances at it. "Since there are only two girls, I thought I would start with them. Besides, ladies are always first in my book."

I can't see his mouth because of the shadow, but I can tell by his eyes that he's smiling.

"Leah and Molly, will you please stand?" They stand. "Leah and Molly, you have both been extended invitations to attend the Tri-State — " Leah and Molly don't let him finish. They shriek, jump into the air, and when they land, hug each other. We all clap. They shriek a second time, throw their arms around Phil, and nearly knock him over.

"Okay." He straightens his hat. "Enough."

"I'm so happy." Leah throws her arms up in the air as if she wants to hug somebody else. The rest of us push closer together on the bench.

"Okay." Phil straightens his hat. He waits for Leah and Molly to sit down, and then he turns and looks at us. "Now, I don't want any of you guys strangling me like Leah and Molly." He shakes his head and then glances at his paper again. "Duncan, Felix, Josh, and Louie, will you please stand — "

"Yes!" Louie leaps into the air, pumping his fist at the sky.

"What about Sam?" I hear Felix shout. "I thought you said Sam was going to make it."

"Well, he did, sort of." I can tell by his voice that he's embarrassed and that he's not smiling. "You guys have been invited to the championships and Sam has been invited to be first alternate."

"Thanks." I swallow the saliva in my mouth. I can feel it slowly dripping down the back of my throat.

"What's an alternate?" someone asks.

"If a kid who's made it to the championships gets hurt, then the alternate takes his place."

"That sucks," Felix shouts.

"He should have made it straight out, Phil," Duncan says. "How come he didn't make it straight out?"

"It's okay, Duncan," I mumble.

"What's going on?" Josh asks. "He should have made it."

"I don't know. Sam came on so fast in the last race maybe they thought it was a fluke. Maybe they wanted to take some of the kids who have done better than Sam all season but just didn't do so well the last race. I don't know."

"It's politics," Duncan says.

"Maybe." Phil folds the paper and stuffs it back in his vest pocket.

"Well, it sucks." Felix stands next to me.

"Those are the breaks, guys," Louie mutters.

"Shut up, Louie, before I show you what breaks," Felix snarls.

"Yeah, you and who else?" Louie brushes past Felix.

"Louie." Phil grabs him by the arm. "You are walking a very thin line."

"I'm only standing up for my rights."

"You don't stand up for your rights by trampling on other people's. You understand what I'm saying?"

"Yeah." Louie pulls his arm away and starts for the lodge.

Phil turns and looks at me. "Hey, Sam, old buddy, don't hang that head. You're first alternate. That's something to be proud of."

*——— **Thirty-two** ———*

I LIE ON my stomach next to the wood-burning stove, my algebra book spread open between my elbows, my chin in my hands, my feet floating over the back of my knees, kicking the floor when I get stuck on the wrong side of an equation. Bo's lying on the sofa. He's holding a folded paperback over his face. I finish the last problem and slap the book closed, relieved that for the first time in a week I've finished the whole set of problems. I roll over on my back, put my feet up on an easy chair, and stare at the cracks in the ceiling. I wonder how long it took them to get there.

"You could always pray."

"What?" I turn and stare at Bo. "What did you say?"

He drops his arms, turns his head sideways, and looks at me. His eyes are so deep set it's as if he's looking out of two caves.

"You could always pray for somebody to get sick or hurt."

"You can't do that."

"Then" — he lifts his book back up in the air — "I'd just forget about it if I were you. Otherwise it's just going to drive you crazy."

That night I sleep so deeply that when I wake in the morning it feels like I'm crawling out of a cave.

* ———— **Thirty-three** ———— *

THE SUN IS an explosion of light and shadow across the snow. The sky is the blue of deep space. Even though it's below freezing, there's no wind and we're wearing only warm-up pants and sweat shirts. No parkas, no hats, no goggles. Just sunglasses and Croakies.

We ride up the chair lift. If we're going to cut school

to ski, this is the day to do it. We get off the lift and glide toward the orange ski patrol sled and bend over to buckle our boots. It's just me, Josh, Duncan, and Felix.

"Was this not a sweet idea?" Felix smiles.

"A day to remember," Duncan adds.

Josh stands up. "As long as we don't get caught."

"How are we going to get caught?"

"I don't know." Josh looks back at the chair lift as if expecting a teacher to get off. "We usually figure out a way."

"You're such a dork." Felix finishes buckling his boots. "We can't do anything without you getting paranoid." He puts his gloves through the straps of his poles and takes off toward the top of Sunrise.

"Don't call me a dork!" Josh shouts after him. "I'm not skiing with anybody that calls me a dork."

"Come on." Duncan taps him on the leg with his pole. "This is supposed to be fun."

"He called me a dork. I'm not going anywhere until he apologizes."

"Ah, come on," Duncan moans. "You're acting like such an old lady."

"Don't you start calling me names."

"I didn't call you names."

"Yes, you did. Apologize."

"I said you're acting like an old lady."

"You did it again. Apologize."

I could have gone to school to hear stuff like this. So I just quietly push myself backward, and when I'm five yards away I turn around and skate. When I come over the lip of the mogul field I see Felix waiting at the cutoff.

I hop through the moguls, getting so high on some jumps that I have to rotate my arms to keep my balance. I head straight for Felix and about twenty yards away turn and spray him with snow. He covers his face with his arm.

"What are you doing?" He flicks the snow off his sweater and pants.

"Sorry." I stand up straight. "I was trying to hit you."

"You would." He takes off his sunglasses. "You messed up my shades, man." He pulls up his sweat shirt and wipes his glasses with the bottom of his turtleneck. "Where are the others?"

"Waiting for you to apologize."

"For what?"

I tell him how they're fighting.

He puts his sunglasses back on, tilts them off his nose, looks under them, and then drops them back down. "Well, in that case let us proceed." He turns his skis downhill and shouts back over his shoulder. "Last one to the bottom buys fries." And he's gone.

I take off after him. I double-pole, skate, and then tuck. When we hit the big curve in the trail I'm beginning to close in on him. That's when the ski patrol in a red parka yells at us through the woods from the next trail.

"Hey, you kids . . ."

We get lower into our tucks and pick up more speed. We come flying out of the big curve to where the trail narrows into a deep chute. Felix hits the chute first. He's about four yards ahead and he's looking back to see if I'm gaining on him. That's when I hear it, the roar of its diesel engine and its spinning turbine. When I come flying over the lip of the chute, I see it pulled across the bottom of the steeps, its silver skin glinting in the sunlight, its barrel pointed up the trail blasting snow straight at us, its tow bar stretched out behind it like a tail. There's no way we can ski past it. I throw my skis sideways and chatter to a stop.

When I look up, Felix is twenty yards from the snow gun and skiing straight into its blizzard.

"Felix," I scream after him. "Stop!"

But he doesn't stop.

Ten yards away from the hitch he begins to come out of his tuck. Five yards away he leaps into the air, his back arched like a ski jumper's. Two yards away his skis are off the snow, high enough to clear the hitch. Then he's over the hitch and he's made it.

I start to breathe again, and as I do the tips of his skis start to rotate. Up in the air. Over his head. Then he's somersaulting backward, cartwheeling through the air out of control. There's a noiseless explosion of skis and poles.

"Felix." His name rips out of my mouth. I kick off my skis and start running down the steeps. I fall and get up and fall again. The snow from the gun is a blizzard of broken glass. I jump over the tow bar, kicking my shin. I see him crumpled in a heap. Not moving.

"Felix." I limp up to him. "Felix."

His skis have broken loose from his boots. I lie down next to him and pull the sweat shirt away from his face. His mouth is bleeding. I wipe his face with the sleeve of my sweat shirt. His face is whiter than snow. His eyes are rolled back under his eyelids. I put my arm under his head. There are flecks of snow in his hair.

"Felix. It's me, Sam. Are you okay?"

He only moans.

"Christ." I look around for a skier, a worker, a ski patrol, anybody, but nobody's near.

His teeth start chattering.

I take off my sweat shirt and wrap it around him like a blanket. What am I going to do? I can't leave him to get help. How can I leave him? No one's coming. I lie down next to him and put my arm back under his head.

Oh, God, please help.

"Help," I call across the mountain. "Please, somebody help."

But there's no one to help. There's only the snow gun and its dumb, stupid roar.

———— Thirty-four ————

WE LIE THERE forever before a ski patrol comes. It's the one with the scraggly black beard. He starts yelling at me as he hikes slowly up the trail toward us.

"You guys can go to jail for skipping school. You know that?" He stops to catch his breath.

"Yeah, well you could be sued for having a snowgun in the middle of an open trail."

"The trail's closed, kid."

"No it isn't."

"Don't argue with me, kid. He better be hurt. That's all I can say." He starts hiking again. "He better not be faking."

"What are you talking about? Look at him!" I shout.

"You're supposed to be helping him. Not yelling at me."

"What do you think I'm doing?" He pants as he takes off his skis. The two-way radio on his belt crackles. He takes it out of his holster. "We're going to need a sled down here at the bottom of Sunrise. That's affirmative." He puts it back in his holster. "Now get out of my way, kid."

I get up and back away, shivering. The sleeves and side of my turtleneck shirt are wet from lying in the snow. I wrap my arms around myself. The two-way radio crackles again in the black holster.

"Sled on its way, over and out."

He doesn't answer, but sticks his skis in the snow so they make an X in front of Felix. Then he kneels next to him and runs his hands over his leg.

"Ow." Felix cries.

"Shit."

"Careful," I shout.

"Will you get out of my face, kid?" He takes out his radio. "We got a major broken leg, Bill. Call the ambulance and get that sled down here, *pronto*. Over."

"Should be there any second. Along with Dorothy and Carl. Let Dorothy handle it. Over."

"Affirmative. Over." He puts the radio back in the holster. "Hold on, kid," he says to Felix. Then to me, "You're racers aren't you?"

"Yeah," I answer, shivering.

"You guys think rules are made to be broken, don't you? Well, this ought to teach you."

For five minutes we stay frozen like that — Felix lying there not moving, me shivering and staring at Felix, the ski patrol kneeling next to him, doing nothing, just kneeling and acting important as if he's getting the ten commandments. I keep looking over my shoulder for the other ski patrol.

When the two of them finally come climbing up the trail with their sled, I call out to them. The guy in the front is pulling the sled with a rope. The woman behind is pushing against a pair of gray steel arms attached to the sled. When they get to Felix, they turn the sled sideways to the hill. The bearded guy gets off his knees and points to Felix's leg. The woman grabs a white splint out of the sled, takes off her gloves, and bends down next to Felix.

"We're just going to brace this leg for you," she whispers in his ear. "It might hurt a little."

She takes the splint and slowly slides it under his leg. It reaches from his hip to his boot.

"Ow," he moans.

"Careful," I say.

"Quiet, kid," the bearded patrol scolds me.

"Almost there." She folds the splint around the sides of his leg and over the top. Then she laces Velcro straps through plastic loops and Velcros them back across his leg.

"There." She blows a strand of hair out of her eyes.

"He's bleeding." I point to his mouth.

She examines the mouth. Then she looks at me and her eyes tell me it's okay. She touches Felix on the cheek with the back of her hand. "We're going to lift you onto the sled. Then it's a free ride down the mountain. It might hurt a little. So you need to be brave."

She points to where she wants the others to lift. Then she puts her gloves on and slides her hands under the splint, and the three of them quickly lift Felix onto the sled.

"Ah," I moan for Felix.

"There." She covers him with a blanket. "That wasn't so bad, was it? Now it's that free ride I promised you."

While she steps into her bindings, she asks the bearded guy to get Felix's skis and poles. He shakes his head as if it's the last thing he should have to do. She backs into the gray handles, reaches behind her back, and grips them with her gloved hands. The other ski patrol grabs his rope. She turns and starts down the mountain, the handles of the sled pressing into the small of her back, her skis edging a wide snowplow. The guy with the rope lets it out slowly until it's taut, then he snowplows after her, braking the sled with the rope.

I watch them creep down the trail. Then I turn and run up to my skis and poles. I throw them over my shoulder and slide down to the snow gun. As I drop them over the tow bar I notice a fat, yellow, electrical cord running from the snow gun into the woods. Without thinking what I'm doing I follow the cord. In the woods the snow is up to my thighs and I trip over hidden branches. The end of the cord is plugged into a socket on the side of a bare electrical pole. I grab the cord with both hands and pull. The plug rips out of the socket. The snow gun sputters and dies.

"There," I say to no one. The last burst of snow falls across the trail and there's silence, except for the roar echoing in my ears.

Thirty-five

I CAN SEE the lights of the ambulance flashing in the pines. The back doors are open, the engine is running. I ski around to the back of the ambulance. It's empty except for a tank of oxygen strapped to the wall. Then the door of the infirmary snaps open and three attendants come hustling out carrying a portable bed. I see the stainless steel frame, the white sheets, and six-inch wheels spinning in the air. All three attendants have matching blue jackets with yellow badges sewn on their left sleeves. They're talking at once.

"Lift it higher." The heavy one with the mustache and glasses is in the front. The other two are in the back.

"His mother is going to be upset," the big blond woman says.

"Of course she's going to be upset," the skinny woman with black hair answers.

"Will you two please lift?" The heavy one places the front of the bed into the ambulance, and the others start to slide it in but a wheel jams.

"Ouch." Felix lifts his head.

"Higher," the heavy one insists.

"Careful," the skinny one answers.

They bend their knees and lift the back of the bed higher.

Felix turns and squints at me, his face white as ice. He half smiles. "Hey."

"Hey, Felix," I answer, happy that he's alive. They slide the bed into the ambulance. I jump in after him.

"Hey, kid, you can't get in there," the heavy guy with the mustache yells at me.

"Just a second." I can't see Felix's face in the dark, but his hand reaches up and grabs my turtleneck.

"I made it." His voice is a whisper.

"Yeah."

"Come on, kid, the sooner you get out the sooner we can get him to the hospital and the sooner the docs can fix his leg."

I try to leave but Felix won't let go.

"You owe me fries," Felix whispers.

"What?"

"Last one down the mountain buys fries." He stops and catches his breath. "I beat you so bad. I had to wait here ten minutes for you."

"But you broke your leg."

"I still beat you by ten minutes."

"Kid."

"Coming." I climb out of the dark into the brilliant light.

"It's about time." The big blond woman climbs in, unfolds a seat off the wall, and sits next to Felix. The others slam the doors and run around to the front. I stand there shivering, staring at the white doors covered with dirt and mud. I can barely make out the word *ambulance* painted in red across the back. The heavy guy revs up the engine and turns on the siren. The back tires spin out, whipping snow and pine needles all over me.

———— Thirty-six ————

WE PARK NEXT to a Mercedes. The woman at the desk tells us he's in room 1028 and to follow the blue line. There are eight colored lines painted on the brown linoleum floor, like an electrical diagram. We follow them. The red line goes right, the rest go straight down the hall. We pass a small room with a cross on the wall. The blue line angles left. We follow it up a stairwell and down a long corridor to where there are numbers on the door. The door to 1028 is open. There's a pink parka thrown over a chair. Mom waits in the hall. I step slowly into the room. Felix's mother is standing next to a curtain that's pulled halfway across the room. She's wearing a gray skirt and white blouse and her hand is on her forehead, as if she's thinking. When she looks up, she notices me.

She smiles. "Sam, how did you get here?"

"My mom."

"Where is she?" She tries to look around me.

"In the hall."

"Well, why don't you come in and visit with Felix? He's sick of me, so I'll go visit your mother." She starts to walk past me. "What's that?" She points to the red carton in my hand.

"Fries for Felix."

"Aren't you nice." She goes out the door.

I step around the gray curtain. Felix is lying there in a hospital bed. He's all in white and his leg is in a white cast hanging from cables and wires. His head is buried in a pillow. His face isn't white anymore. It's more the yellow of a bruise after it fades.

"Hey, Felix."

"Sam," he whispers.

"I brought you fries," I whisper back.

"Thanks."

"They're a little cold."

"That's okay."

"I got ketchup, too." I show him the plastic packs of ketchup in my other hand.

"Thanks."

"Does it hurt?"

"Yeah."

"I mean, more than before?"

"Yeah."

I blow air between my lips. "How long until you're better?"

"I can't walk for six weeks. I can't ski until next year."

"Whew." I whistle. "Not until next year?"

"If I'm lucky."

"You'll be lucky."

"I broke my leg, man. You call that lucky?"

I don't know what to say. His voice makes me sad and nervous. I look down at the fries in one hand and the plastic packs of ketchup in the other. I bite open one of the packs and squeeze the ketchup over the fries.

"Here." I hand him one of the ketchup-covered fries. He eats it slowly. I hand him another one.

"No." He puts up a hand. "You eat them. I can't."

"I can't eat them. They're yours."

"Sam." He turns his head on his pillow. The whites of his eyes are yellow. "You brought them for me."

"Yeah."

"So they're mine and I can do with them what I want." He lifts his head.

"Yeah."

"I don't want them. Do me a favor and eat them."

"But I brought them for you."

"Then throw them away."

"I'm not throwing them away."

"Then eat them."

"Okay, I'll eat them. I just feel like a jerk eating the fries I brought you."

"Sam." He puts his head down on his pillow. "How come you feel like a jerk if you're doing me a favor?"

———— Thirty-seven ————

EVERY TIME I CLOSE my eyes there's the roar of the snow gun. Felix is cartwheeling backward through the sky and I'm running down the mountain, the snow from the gun burning my face like tears. The bearded face of the ski patrol fills the sky like a storm cloud. I wake to his thundering laugh. Even with a pillow over my head, I keep hearing the roar. I keep seeing Felix fall.

When I look at the clock it's only twelve-thirty. Morning is never going to come. I get out of bed. The house is dark. I walk into Mom's room. She's lying on her back, her arm over her head. What am I going to say if I wake her? That I'm having bad dreams? I'm not a little kid. I go down the dark stairs and open the icebox. The light flashes across the room as if it's taking a picture. I don't know what I'm looking for. I squint at a gallon of milk and a carton of orange juice. I take the blue cap off the milk, purse my lips to the top, and take a long drink. It goes down like something solid. I close the door and the kitchen is swallowed back into darkness.

I walk slowly back to the living room, feeling my way with my bare feet on the cold floor. I sit in front of the piano and stare through the dark at the keyboard. The white keys are broken up like shadows in a mogul field. Without touching them, I start playing a song. I can feel the music. I don't remember my fingers touching the keys. When evening falls this hard I remember only the sound of Felix's leg breaking. The woman wrapping his leg in white Velcro and pain all around. The ambulance lighting up the pines. My voice like a bridge of withered flowers. Someone is standing by my side. A hand settles over mine. I stop playing.

"Pretty."

"Yes."

"It's time to lay you down," she whispers. "It's nearly one."

"Yeah." When I stand up I try not to look in her eyes. She wraps her arms around me.

"I got to go to bed." I try and get around her, but she won't let go.

"I'm sorry about Felix."

"Yeah."

"I wish my words could comfort you. I wish I could tell you that I could make Felix better. It breaks a mother's heart to see her son so sad. But there's nothing that will make his leg better, except time."

She touches my cheek with her hand. "It hurts when someone you care about gets hurt and there's nothing you can do except comfort him."

She puts her arm around my waist. "But that's all we can do for Felix and that's all I can do for you. Come on, let's go to bed."

We walk slowly through the living room and up the stairs.

"Sometimes," she whispers, "the only comfort we have is knowing that all we can do is give comfort. I know that doesn't feel like enough, but everything else is out of our hands."

She turns off my light and kisses me on the forehead. Her cheek is wet. "Good night, sweetheart."

"Good night, Mom." I roll over onto my side. When I fall asleep I dream that Mom and I are bringing Felix down the mountain on a sled. His leg is suspended in the air like a bridge.

——— Thirty-eight ———

"GUYS," PHIL SHOUTS at us, "this is not a Mickey Mouse course!" He points with his ski pole at the red bamboo gates. We have to squint into the bright sun. "Contrary to what you may think, you cannot ski this course like Mickey Mouse. Not even you, Louie."

We're not sure if we're supposed to laugh or not. What he said is funny, but how he shouted wasn't. We kind of look at each other without looking at each other, and then we just nod and try to keep from smiling.

"Now, I understand how some of you might be confused by the bright sun and the heat of the day. I can see how you might have thought for a minute that you were in Disney World. But this course is no Magic Kingdom. In fact, it's nowhere near the Magic Kingdom. You can't run a race course, guys, and have your minds thousands of miles away. I guarantee you, it's impossible."

Yeah. We all nod. It's impossible.

"Now, before we start again I want you guys to do me a favor. I want you to grab the invisible handle sticking out of your right ear." He holds his hand up to his ear. "And I want you to start cranking." He rotates his fist as if turning a crank.

We don't look at each other. We just look at him and start cranking our hands in small circles next to our ears.

"Good. You guys know what you're doing? You're reeling your brains back into your heads. You can stop cranking when you hear that dull, clunking sound. That's the noise your brains make when they get locked back into place."

One by one we stop cranking.

"Good. Now, how many of you guys have visited Felix?"

Molly, Duncan, and I raise our hands.

"What about the rest of you? He sure could use some company. His mother tells me he's got at least another week in there, so you should all visit him." He points to the chair lift. "Now let's ski."

We turn and start gliding toward the chair lift.

"Sam," Phil calls after me.

What? I jam my skis sideways and stop.

"Come here."

I herringbone back up the hill. My skis slip so I turn sideways and sidestep. When I get up to him I'm breathing hard. The sun is over his shoulder.

"I got a call last night and you're in the championships."

"That's because of Felix."

"It's because of a lot of things."

"I don't want to go."

"You don't want to go because Felix broke his leg. Do you think Felix doesn't want you to go?"

"I don't know."

"Why don't you ask him?"

"Yeah, well, I didn't make it."

"Hey, Sam, this isn't the Magic Kingdom. This isn't pretend. This is real life. This is racing. We have alternates because kids get sick and kids get hurt. You should be proud to be the first alternate. And you should be proud that you've been invited to the championships. Do you understand what I'm saying?"

"Yeah, but . . ."

"No yeahs, buts. The championships are next week. We have today and tomorrow to get ready. Now get up there and ski."

"Yeah, but . . ."

"Get your buts up the mountain and ski."

I turn and start gliding down the mountain again. I veer off toward the edge of the trail where a snow gun has been pulled to the side. As I pass it I jab the pointed end of my ski pole at the stainless steel skin, wishing it had a heart so I could plunge my pole straight into it.

✳———— Thirty-nine ————✳

WE GO IN for lunch. It's crowded. I look all over for Bo. He's not upstairs at the table where we put our stuff. I take off my boots and slip into my running shoes. I have to reach over a couple of bodies and under a table to grab the gray and white igloo. I slide open the top and pull out a juice box and a sandwich bag. Turkey and bean sprouts on hearty wheat. I open the bag. Mayonnaise drips over my fingers. I lick them clean and take a bite. The sprouts taste like horse hairs. The thought makes me almost gag. I jab the straw in the juice box and take a long pull. Apple cranberry. I keep glancing up, looking for Bo. I open the hearty wheat and start picking out the sprouts. They're gunky with mayonnaise and come out in a glob. I'm putting the glob in a plastic bag when I see Bo coming down the aisle toward me.

"Yo, Sam." He slaps my hand, then puts out his huge palm for me to slap. He messes up my hair. "How's it feel?"

"How'd you know?"

"Word gets around the mountain fast."

"Who told you?"

"One of the lift attendants."

"Bull."

"Phil told me. Move over and give me a sandwich. He said you were being a jerk."

"I am not being a jerk." I slide over to the next chair.

"He said you didn't want to go." He starts taking off his boots.

"I don't."

"That's not being a jerk?"

"I'm not a jerk."

He looks up at me from his boots. "Hand me a sandwich."

I reach into the igloo and pull out a sandwich. He sits up and takes it.

"You're a jerk if Felix is the reason you don't want to go. That's ridiculous."

"Why is that ridiculous?"

"Because there are two other kids that got hurt and can't go."

"What do you mean? Phil never told me that."

"Phil doesn't know what a sensitive jerk you are, so he didn't tell you. You know what that means?"

I don't say anything.

"It means there are two other alternates that are going. It means you're not taking Felix's place. You're taking another kid's place."

* —————— Forty —————— *

"MOM, WE'RE GOING to the movies," I yell up the stairs.

"Who's we?" she calls back from her room.

"Me and Bo."

"And how do you suppose you're going to get there?"

"Miranda."

"What time are you going to be home?"

"Not late."

"What is that supposed to mean? You both have practice tomorrow. You probably shouldn't even go."

"We're visiting Felix, too."

"You're visiting Felix?" She comes out of her room and leans over the banister, her hair falling around her face. "Just don't be too late."

——— Forty-one ———

"SO HOW WAS the movie?" Felix clicks off the television. He's sitting in a wheelchair and wearing blue pajamas. His cast is hanging from a metal rod.

"Your basic movie," Bo answers. "Guns, cars, kisses, and karate."

"Sounds good." Felix smiles his white-enamel smile.

"It was bad," Miranda says. "As bad as the popcorn, which was soft, soggy, and squeaked when you bit into it."

"Squeaky popcorn." Felix shudders. "That's worse than fingernails on blackboards."

"Worse than slicing a finger sharpening skis," Bo adds.

"I hate slicing my finger," Miranda moans.

"Worse than breaking your leg," Felix adds.

"Right." We all nod sarcastically.

"I can't stand squeaky popcorn."

"You can't stand on a broken leg, either," Bo scolds.

"How is your leg?" Miranda asks. "Is it getting better?"

"Yeah, it's getting better. I'm just getting sick of this place. I guess I just got the hospital blues."

"We can get you stuff," Miranda offers. "Magazines, paperbacks — "

"No books! Please, no books. My mother's gotten every homework assignment that's due for the next ten years. Every time she comes in she wants to know what page I'm on. She says this is my chance to get ahead, to develop a thirst for knowledge."

"If you're thirsty, why doesn't she bring you a Coke?" Bo asks.

Felix nods. "Now that's a good idea."

"We'll get you a Coke." Miranda pulls Bo's arm. "There's a machine down the hall."

"Get me one, too." In the reflection of the window I watch them disappear, then I watch Felix turn and look at me.

"What are you so quiet about?"

"Nothing," I answer his reflection.

"Why don't you tell me the good news?"

"About what?"

"About the championships."

"How'd you know?"

"Phil. He comes in every day."

"Phil comes in every day?"

"Yeah, he brings me *Playboy*s and — "

"He does not bring you *Playboy*s."

"How do you know?"

"I know."

"Yeah, well, we're not talking about that. We're talking about your good news."

"It's not good news."

"Since when is making the championships not good news?"

"I didn't make the championships. I'm an alternate."

"You're not an alternate. Alternates don't go to the championships."

"I am too an alternate. It's just because you and others got hurt that I'm going."

"So?"

"So it's not the same as making it."

"Wake up, Sam. Who cares that you were an alternate? Who cares that I got hurt? The fact is, you're going and I'm not."

"I care."

"What do you care about? That you were an alternate or that I can't go?"

"Both."

"Yeah, well, I can't go," he snaps. "And that's that. Did it ever occur to you that since I can't go that I might want a friend to go in my place?"

"No."

"What if you got hurt and I got to go to the championships instead of you? Wouldn't that make you feel okay?"

"Yeah, but I'd tell you that it makes me feel okay."

"That's what I'm trying to tell you, you jerk."

"Then why don't you say so?"

"Sam, if I wasn't in this wheelchair, I'd kick you in the head with my cast."

Forty-two

WE BUCKLE OUR BOOTS at the top of the Eastern. There's a river of fog down in the valley, but up here we're above the clouds. The sun is shining. Tiny birds are singing in the hardwoods, flitting from tree to tree. The air is still. The sun is warm on our parkas.

"Okay, guys, listen up." Phil adjusts his goggles. "This is our last practice before the championships. We've worked hard all winter and we worked really hard yesterday, so today we're just going to free ski."

"Yeah!" we all yell together.

"We're going to ski top to bottom and we're going to ski fast. I want you guys to feel speed. I want you to think speed."

"Yeah!" we shout again.

"The faster you ski the faster things happen. And the faster things happen the faster you have to think." He makes that cranking motion to the side of his head. "You understand?"

We nod.

"Good. Now watch." He double-poles into the steeps. When he makes his first turn his inside arm almost scrapes the mountain. His skis carve through the snow like skates. His upper body stays still, his hips swivel, his legs swing as smoothly as a pendulum. He stops at the halfway mark.

"Who's first?" Leah asks.

"Why not the alternate?" Louie asks.

Leah squints at him. "You know, I'm tired of your

put-downs, and if I'm tired of them, I wonder how Sam feels."

"Hey, what I say? I didn't say anything that wasn't the truth. He's an alternate."

"Louie's just scared that Sam's going to beat him," Josh says.

"Oh, make me puke. You're the one shitting in his pants, afraid I'm going to beat you."

"Louie." Duncan points down the trail. "Phil's waving at you. He wants you to go first."

"Yeah." He sticks his fist in the air. "And the first shall be first."

Right. We watch him push himself over the edge. He doesn't double-pole, and when he turns, you can tell that his skis are sliding out by the snow spraying into the air. When it's my turn I adjust my goggles, check my bindings, and double-pole into the steeps. I have to catch my breath, it's so steep. It's like jumping off a roof. I force myself forward. I get going so fast that my parka snaps in the wind and air whips underneath my goggles, making my eyes tear. I try to ski like Phil, but I know I'm slipping on some of my turns by the scraping sounds my skis make. When I hit the flats I tuck, my head bouncing just over my knees, my hands out in front of my head.

At the bottom I get on the chair with Josh. We don't say much. We just sit there looking down at the snow melting off our skis, the water beading on the plastic surface. An old guy with dark glasses and a cigar sticking out of his mouth skis underneath us. A pack of little kids scream past him.

It takes only fifty seconds to race top to bottom. Not

a lot of time to think. Not a lot of time to make up for mistakes. It takes ten minutes to ride bottom to top, a lot of time to think about the mistakes I made on the way down and to look into the bare hardwoods along the edges of the trail. Toward the end of the morning it gets so warm that the snow begins to soften. It's easier to carve turns in soft snow than on ice, but by the time we make our last run, the snow is too soft and too full of water. At the top of the mountain the air smells like the ocean, and the water in the snow glistens like water on a beach when the waves wash away.

I wait at the top of Eastern while the others take their last run. Then I double-pole over the edge. Halfway into the steeps I hit a mound of manmade snow as I turn, and it throws me slightly off balance. As I carve back across the mountain, the wet snow grabs my downhill ski and starts tracking me straight into the hardwoods. I try to transfer my weight over the ski to control it, but it won't be controlled. I panic and throw my weight into the mountain. I fall, rip out of my bindings, and skid through small pines into the hardwoods. Branches tear off my hat and goggles and scratch my face. Wet snow plows up my cuffs and my waist. I finally come to a stop with my face pressed against a white birch.

"Shit." I feel my arms and legs. Nothing's broken, nothing's even bruised. I take a deep breath and slowly wrap my arms around the white, papery bark of the birch and pull myself out of the wet snow. I try to shake the snow out of my cuffs and waist. Some of it drips down my legs. I trudge out the trail I plowed, slowly gathering my hat and goggles and skis.

By the time I get to the race shack everyone else is in

street clothes and Phil is giving us his final lecture of
the season.

"Go home and do what has to get done. Get to bed
early tonight and every night this week. Study hard and
make sure that on Saturday your skis are sharp and
waxed and that you are sharp and ready to go. Any
questions?"

Nobody says anything.

"Okay, it was a good workout. I'm glad to see we had
a few falls. This is the time and place to get them out
of your system. If you're going to fall, fall in practice."

No one laughs or says anything, not even Louie. We
just stand there, our faces grim.

"Hey, dudes." Phil shakes his head. "Lighten up.
You're going to the championships, not the electric
chair."

——— Forty-three ———

I PUSH THE PILE of blankets and sheets off to the side
and sit down on the end of Bo's bed.

"Hey, don't mess up my bed." He kicks the covers off
his feet. He's stretched out on his bed with his clothes
on, his head propped up against the headboard, reading
Mad magazine. "How am I supposed to keep my room
picked up with slobs like you messing it up?"

"Funny."

"Not when Mom's yelling at you." He looks over the magazine at me.

"All right, I'm sorry. I only came in to ask you something."

"Ask me anything, just don't mess up my room."

"What's it like — "

"It's hell, just like when she's yelling at you." He kicks a shirt onto the floor. I watch it settle over a pair of pants and a sweater.

"I'm not asking you about your room. I'm asking you what the championships are like."

"Intense."

"What does that mean?"

"It means," he lowers the magazine, "intense. Intense means exciting, stimulating, overwhelming. The whole world's at the championships. There are thousands of racers, thousands of coaches, thousands of parents . . ."

"Thousands?"

"Okay, hundreds. Hundreds of racers, hundreds of coaches, hundreds of parents. And there are reps there. You'll see their vans in the parking lot with logos painted on the sides. The whole world is there." He picks up the magazine again.

"Weren't you nervous?"

"Nervous? Yeah, of course I was nervous."

"I know I'm going to be nervous. I'm already nervous."

"At least you're talking about it. I'll tell you something, every other kid there will be nervous." He throws the magazine on the floor and sits up. "Being nervous is part of it. So you might as well get used to it."

"Yeah?"

"Yeah. When I get nervous the back of my legs always start trembling."

"Mine too."

"Kind of like a car idling. Anyway, that's what I keep telling myself when I get nervous. That I'm just like a car idling, waiting for the light to turn green. And the only thing that's going to make the idling stop is for me to put it in gear and step on the pedal. I try to get myself to a point where I can't wait to blast out of the start and race down the mountain. You understand what I'm saying?"

"Sort of."

"Nerves are weird, but you want to know what the weirdest part is?"

"What?"

"The weirdest part is that the championships are something every racer works for all winter, right? This is where we all want to be."

I nod my head.

"If we don't make it to the championships, we act like it's the end of the world, but the weird part is that when we do make it, we act like it's the end of the world."

"Yeah. How come we're so weird?"

"You're asking me why people are weird?"

"Yeah."

"I don't have a clue." He shrugs his shoulders and then a smile curls across his lips. "Maybe we should write to Ann Landers. Think she would know?"

"I doubt it."

✳———— Forty-four ————✳

THAT NIGHT I DREAM that the clock radio is talking to me. The red numbers flicker four-thirty in the dark.

"Morning, Sam. We early hours don't usually get to see you. To what do we owe this honor? Are you interested in learning about the subtleties of time? You've come to the right place. We're the professors of time." The numbers flicker.

I smack the top of the clock.

"Wrong button, Sam. That's the doze button. Dozing speeds up time. Concentrating slows down time. If you can slow down time you can win races. Are you paying attention, Sam? Races are won by concentrating."

I smack the doze button again, roll over, and pull the pillow over my head.

"Sam, it's six-thirty. Time to get up."

"Huh?" I pull the pillow off my head and try to open my eyes, but my eyelids are sealed with sleep. I rub them until I can look across the room. Mom is standing in the doorway in her nightgown.

"Time to get up." She starts to leave.

"Wait." I look at the clock sitting on my bedside table.

"I'm waiting. What's up?"

"I don't know if I want to go."

"You know the rules."

"I don't mean school. I mean I don't know if I want to go to the championships."

"Ah." She sits down on the side of my bed. "And why don't you know if you want to go?"

"I don't know. Bo says it's really intense."

"And you can't handle that?"

"I don't know."

"You're going to have some disappointed teammates."

I yawn.

"A disappointed coach."

I cover my mouth and look at the wall.

"A disappointed brother and a disappointed mother."

"You don't even come to my races. If you don't come to my races, how can you be disappointed?"

"I don't come to your races because you don't want me to."

"Because you don't care."

"Sam, that is — " She stops and puts a hand on my cheek. "Of course I care. Would you like me to come to this race with you?"

"You mean the championships?"

"Yes, I mean the championships."

"I don't know."

"I'd like to come."

"What about Bo?"

"He can come too."

"He has a race."

"Well, Bo can go to his race. It's not a championship, is it?"

"No."

"And I'll go to yours."

Forty-five

"YOU'VE GOT TO treat your skis like your best friend. If you were old enough I'd tell you that you've got to treat them the way you treat your girl."

"Shut up, Bo. I'm old enough."

I turn on the light, and the naked bulb hanging from an old timber shines across the workbench. It's covered with orange, red, blue, and purple wax drippings. Bo picks up my K2s, separates them, and lays them on the workbench. He plugs in the iron, reaches into a basket, and grabs a bar of blue wax. He holds the tip of the iron over the skis and touches the wax to the iron. The wax melts and Bo drips it along the length of each ski. The room fills with smoke.

"Too hot." He yanks out the plug. "Open the window."

I open the frost-covered window a crack. When I turn back, Bo is running the iron along the length of the black bottoms like he's ironing a pair of pants. Then he picks up a blue scraper and scrapes the skis from the tips. The wax peels off like layers of onion skin. He holds up a layer.

"See that?" The ribbon of wax is flecked with dirt. "That's what'll slow you down." He hands me the scraper. "Your turn."

When I'm through I wipe the skis with a paper towel. Then Bo takes a smooth black stone and rubs it along the metal edges. He gets down low to blow the stone dust off. Then he takes a file, and holding it at an angle, pulls it partway down the ski. He goes over the same area three or four times. The file leaves a trail of metal tailings. He wipes the bottoms off with a paper towel and continues filing until he gets to the end of the ski. Then he turns the ski on its side and runs the file along the edges.

"Feel this."

I rub a fingernail over the edge. It leaves a film of fingernail powder on the cold metal.

"Sharp," I mumble.

"That's so you can turn on ice. Call the weather station and get tomorrow's temperature."

I go into the kitchen and dial *w-e-a-t-h-e-r*. I have to listen about a full-service bank, how I can sign up to lose twenty pounds, and why I need extra life insurance, before I get the report. It's going to be partly sunny and between twenty-five and forty degrees. I tell Bo. He looks up at the colored wax chart on the wall.

"Purple and red." He reaches into the basket, takes out a purple bar and two reds, presses them together, and plugs in the iron. He drips the purple and red wax onto the bottoms and then irons the wax so that it runs evenly into all the pores. Even with the window open the air fills with the smell of wax.

Bo leans the skis against the wall with the bottoms facing us.

"Thanks, Bo," I say, touching the warm bottoms of the skis. "This wax smell reminds me of something."

"Church," Bo says, putting his skis down on the workbench. "This place always reminds me of church."

Forty-six

MORNING COMES LIKE a glacier. I get out of bed in the dark and take a shower. It's so cold I pull on my long underwear in the bathroom. Steam swirls around the light, the mirror is fogged over. Downstairs the wood-burning stove is roaring. Bo is in the kitchen, standing next to the stove, a coffee cup in one hand, a spatula in the other. Blue flames flicker underneath a black frying pan.

"Morning," he says.

"Morning." I pull the carton of orange juice out of the icebox and take a long drink.

"Use a glass."

"Sorry." I put the carton back.

After breakfast I go outside to start the truck. I slide into the frozen driver's seat, put my foot on the clutch, jiggle the gear shift into neutral, and turn the key. The engine grinds, turns over, and starts. I rev it up so the tachometer reads twelve hundred. I hold it there and count to sixty the way Bo taught me. Then I take my foot off the accelerator and crank on the heat.

On the way back inside I notice that the dark is lightening. The sky is crisp and clear. There is a moon. And there are stars bright enough to shine through the moonlight. If these stars had voices they would have the voices of birds. And all around me the trees would be waking to their songs.

✳——— Forty-seven ———✳

WE DROP BO OFF at Thunder Mountain. We hug each other good-bye for good luck, then Mom and I follow Phil over the mountain and down into a wide valley. The road winds along a river, steam misting off the water. Behind us, the rising sun cuts through the steam and lights up the frost-covered trees. And then, all of a sudden, the frost starts breaking away from the branches and floating through the air like snowflakes that are the size of silver dollars.

I lean back in my seat and close my eyes. The warm air from the heater blows on my legs. The warmth of the sun is on my shoulders. I don't remember falling asleep. If I did sleep I dreamed of snowflakes lit up by sunlight.

The truck rocks on its shocks as we crawl over the frozen ruts of a parking lot.

"Here we are," Mom says, parking next to a van with a K2 logo painted on the side. I look out through the windshield. The mountain looks cold and white from the top to the bottom, where it's surrounded by gray condominiums.

When she turns off the engine I feel another engine take up its idle. This is it. I take a deep breath, trying to control my nerves. Lighten up. This is where I want to be. I loosen my neck. Relax, you're going to the championships, not the electric chair.

Forty-eight

IT'S MORE LIKE a trembling than an idling, just under the skin at the back of my knees. I stand behind Josh waiting to get my bib. On the wall behind the registration table is a big sign that says Welcome to the Junior III Tri-State Championships. It's only eight o'clock in the morning, but already the lodge is packed with thousands of racers, thousands of coaches, thousands of parents. There are so many people talking at once that I can hum a song and not hear myself. Over by our table I can see Mom reading a book as if it's just another day. Suddenly Josh isn't in front of me and there's a gray-haired woman smiling across the table at me. Her face isn't as old as her hair.

"Good morning. Your name, please."

I give her my name and my USSA card. She hands me a bib with a Coca-Cola logo on it. I open it. I'm number seventy-three.

"Good luck," she says. "Next."

"Thanks." I walk over to the leader board. There are seventy-five racers. At least I'm not last. I fold the bib and walk back to our table. The rest of the guys are pulling on their GS suits. I zip open my ski bag, take out my boots and socks, my blue slalom pants, and my red and white slalom sweater. I put my boots on last. I unsnap the buckles, pull the tongue toward the toe, stick in my foot, stand up, and stomp the boot on the floor until my foot squeezes into the liner. When I look up the other guys are zipping on their warm-ups and Phil is standing at the door. I grab my warm-ups and wrap them around my waist, but when I reach down to zip up one of the legs, the waist falls down. I pull them back up and try again. Again they fall down. My hands are trembling.

"Here." Two hands hold the warm-ups to my waist. I reach down, attach the double zipper, and pull it up. The pant leg zips closed. Then I do the other leg. The waist holds.

"There." Mom takes her hands away.

"Thanks." I pull on my parka and zip it up. I pull on my bib, hat, goggles, and gloves.

"I'll see you out there," Mom says.

"Yeah." I take a deep breath.

We hike up the mountain. The sky is blue and the moon is still floating in it like a white cloud. The snow is sprinkled with stars. By the time we get to the starting line, I'm sweating, and the trembling has settled into a quiet idle. A blue finish line is painted across the snow. A white cloth banner hanging from a cable over the finish line flutters lightly in the wind. Printed in big red letters across the front is Junior III Tri-State Championships. They don't let you forget for a minute where you are. We cross the finish line and start hiking up the course. At the fourth gate Phil stops. We unzip our parkas.

"There are no more tomorrows, guys. This is it. You have to pay attention. Now look down these last four gates. I want you to take as straight a line as you can through them. You can tuck; just remember to roll your skis on edge. Memorize what you see. I want you to memorize this course so you could ski it if you were blind." He turns and starts hiking.

We follow him as always, up through the gates. Other racers are snowplowing down through the course, and as usual we're the only racers hiking. Every four gates he stops and tells us exactly how he wants us to ski them. By the time we get to the top, our parkas are tied around our waists. We stand there, sweating, breathing hard, leaning on our poles, looking down the course filled with racers.

"Burn it into your memories, guys."

I try and follow the course as it snakes down to the finish line — red, blue, red, blue, red, blue. Steep at the top. Flattening out a little. Steep again. Then the flats and the final dip into the last ten gates.

"Forty-four gates; twenty-two blues, twenty-two reds. You guys can deal with that number. You can memorize that many turns."

We study the course without saying a word. We're as quiet as if we're in a church.

"Okay, we'll snowplow through it. Then we'll come up on the chair."

We snake through the course. Phil stops at an undergate.

"Sam, how do you ski this red undergate?"

I look at the blue gate above it. The problem with the undergate is that it makes you think you have to turn when you don't. All you have to do is hold your turn through the blue into the red. Instead of making two turns, you make only one turn. I explain it to him.

"Good. You got that, guys? Is there anything else about this gate?"

"Yeah, there's a bump in the middle of it," Leah says.

"That's right. And what do we do with bumps when we're racing?"

"We suck them up," we all answer.

"Exactly," Phil says. "Bend those knees like shock absorbers." He bends his knees quickly so he's in a tuck and then standing up again. "Has to be that quick." He turns and starts down the mountain. The whole way down I memorize gate after gate. It's easier than memorizing vocabulary words. At the bottom we cross the finish line. Mom is standing off to the side. She's wearing Bo's old green parka and his torn purple warm-ups with gray duct-tape patches over the rear. I wave at her as we pass. She waves back. The trembling is definitely an idle now.

* ——— Forty-nine ——— *

WE TAKE A COUPLE of free runs. Phil leads the way. He makes wide, sweeping GS turns. After our second run I end up in line with Louie. We glide in front of the oncoming chair. The attendant holds it while we start to sit down. He lets it go and the chair swoops forward, lifting us toward the first tower. I pull down the safety bar.

"Easy course." Louie is the first to speak.

"Yeah," I say looking down at the snow dripping off the white skin of my skis.

"I'm going to break the top ten today. I can just feel it."

"Yeah?"

"I got a real good start today. I'm thirty-seven. What are you?"

"Seventy-three."

"Ooph." He blows air through his fat lips as if he can't believe bib numbers go that high. "You're going to have to really ski to move up today."

"Yeah." I have a sudden urge to throw him off the chair. But when I look over the side, we're going up over a pile of rocks. If I threw him off here he'd be dead and I would end up in the electric chair. It'd be better if I just punched him, but I don't even do that. I just say, "Yeah."

"Yeah, seriously. There are a lot of seriously good racers today. No wannabes here today. You'll be lucky to get into the sixties."

"Yeah, well, wish me luck," I say sarcastically.

"Yeah," he answers, as if he's never heard sarcasm before. "Good luck, man."

Fifty

IT'S LIKE A CIRCUS at the top of the mountain. The sun has gotten so warm that everybody has taken off their parkas. The girls' nylon GS suits are the bright colors of swimsuits. All the coaches are wearing brightly colored shirts with neck zippers and designer labels. Everyone's wearing sunglasses. Some girls are putting colored lip balm on their lips, cheeks, and noses. Skis and poles and parkas are spread across the snow. We find a place by the woods where we can take off our skis. We pile our jackets in the shade, then go over to watch Molly and Leah.

There's a crowd of racers lined up all the way down to the fourth gate. We squeeze into the crowd near the third gate.

"Leah go yet?" I ask.

"She's next," Josh answers.

I squint up at the starting house. It's so dark under the eaves that all I can see is Leah's light hair. I know Phil is somewhere behind her.

The guys start chanting, "Leah, Leah, Leah."

And then she comes shooting out of the dark. We cheer and click our poles together as she disappears into the steeps. We stay and cheer Molly, then go over and start getting our skis ready. I let the other guys scrape their skis first. When they're through, I take a blue scraper and my skis and find a shaded place in the woods where the snow is firm enough to stand on. As the purple and red wax peels off, I start thinking about Bo. He's probably on course right now. I stand up and try to figure out the direction that Thunder Mountain is in and shout, "Good luck, Bo."

"Thanks," the guys shout back at me.

I look at them between the shadows and saplings. "I was shouting good luck to Bo."

"Good luck to you, too."

"Thanks." I bend over the skis again, wipe my eyes with the cuff of my sweater, and continue scraping. "Good luck, Bo," I say every time I complete a stroke, like an offering. "Good luck, Bo. Good luck, brother." By the time I finish, the girls are gone and Duncan and Josh are stripped down to their GS suits and clicked into their bindings. Phil has his hands on their shoulders. Every time he makes a point he raises his voice. Then he slaps them on the fanny and they skate over to the starting shack. I go down to where we watched Leah and Molly. One by one the guys start coming out of the dark. When Duncan and Josh go, I click my poles and shout so loud my throat gets scratchy. They both look good. Duncan is higher than usual, but he snaps through his turns. Josh is low and cat quick. When I go back to our place, Louie is stretching against a tree and Phil's talking to him.

I sit down, and when Louie heads for the start I don't move. Why should I? I watch him get in line behind the starting house. Phil is patting him on the back and whispering in his ear. I get up, grab my poles, and slowly walk to the second gate. It won't hurt just to watch. Number thirty-five is stiff and slow, as if he's been sitting in front of a television. Number thirty-six is just the opposite. He's in such a hurry he misses the fourth gate completely. The idle picks up. I start clicking my poles and whistling. When number thirty-seven slashes out of the darkness into the sunlight, I can't help cheering.

"Go, Louie!" I yell him over the crest and into the steeps.

I turn around and start back for our coats. Forty more racers to go. Another forty minutes to wait. I sit down on the pile of coats. There are many things about this sport I haven't figured out yet. One is all the waiting. I get up at five in the morning and drive two hours to a mountain to climb and memorize a course. Then I wait for all the girls to go. Then all of the boys. And after all that waiting, I'm on the course for only fifty seconds. Fifty seconds. After all that waiting, all those hours of practicing, all those hours of driving, I have only fifty seconds on the course. I kick my heels and snow sprays up and around my yellow boots. Felix has to wait six weeks before he can walk. Six months before he can run. A year before he can ski. A pair of skis sprays to a stop in front of my boots. I look up. It's Duncan. Right behind him is Josh. I jump to my feet.

"How'd you do?"

"Okay. Listen." Duncan's voice is really serious. "You know where you go into the last ten gates, where it drops? The second gate is really tight. You'll be carrying so much speed from the flats, that turn comes quicker than you think. I almost blew it."

"Me too," Josh adds.

"A lot of kids are blowing it out there. So be ready."

"Yeah." I'll be ready. I try to picture the gate he's talking about. The second gate into the final dip?

Phil whistles from the start. "Sam." I look at him. He makes a sign with his fingers for me to run and stretch.

"Good luck." Josh and Duncan grab their stuff. "We'll be cheering."

"Yeah." I start running up the mountain. The snow

is soft and slippery. I kick my toes into the snow as I run. What gate are they talking about? The second gate just into the dip? Is it a left turn or a right turn? Damn, I thought I had memorized it better. When I kick the snow it feels like I'm kicking someone in the ribs. Who? I run up the slope. Be ready. Left or right? I should have asked them to explain it better. Why didn't I ask them? I'm such a jerk. I stop running. My side aches like I've been kicked in the ribs. I turn around and ski down the slope on the soles of my boots, breathing hard, looking out over the mountains — barren white with brown trees.

When I get back to my coat, I lean against a tree to stretch the muscles in the back of my legs. Then I dig my skis out of the snow, bring them out of the woods, and clean them with the back of my gloves. When I look up Phil is walking toward me, and right next to him is Mom. Her face is flushed and she's carrying Bo's green parka and purple warm-ups over her shoulder.

* —————— **Fifty-one** —————— *

"IT'S SO HOT they're stopping to salt the course," Phil says.

"Salt the course?" Mom asks. "Why would they do a thing like that?"

"To make me wait longer," I say.

"The snow's gotten too slow and too mushy. The salt

will freeze it up. Give me your skis, Sam. We have about twenty minutes. I want to get some paraffin on your bottoms." Phil takes a white block of wax out of his hip bag and flips my skis over. The black bottoms are beaded with water. He takes a small terry cloth towel out of his bag and wipes the bottoms. Then he rubs the wax into the skis. He talks as he rubs, his voice jerky from exertion.

"We don't want . . . any of the warm snow . . . slowing you down. . . . This paraffin will wick the water away . . . so that you will fly. . . . Did you tune these?" He stops to feel the edges.

"Me and Bo."

"You guys" — he starts rubbing the wax in again — "did a great job. . . . We're going to make these babies . . . so fast." He puts the wax back in his pack and takes out a piece of cork the size of a fist. He rubs the wax into the ski with the flat side of the cork. "Because we . . . don't have . . . an iron . . . we have to use friction . . . to create heat. . . . We want this wax . . . in every pore in the ski. . . . You have to . . . rub . . . and rub . . . and rub." He stops to catch his breath and wipe the sweat off his forehead. Then he starts rubbing again. "It's a sport of details, Sam . . . little details. . . . Paying attention . . . to the little details . . . is what . . . makes . . . a . . . champion. . . . There." He takes a blue scraper out of his pocket and starts scraping the wax. "Sam . . . while I'm . . . doing this . . . stretch out."

I pick up my coat and spread it out.

"Here." Mom picks up my coat. "Use this." She spreads Bo's coat out over the snow. I sit down on the old green parka. It puffs up around my legs. White feathers peek out of little holes. I stick my left leg straight out in front of me, my right leg bent at right angles to my side. Then I lean forward as if flying over a hurdle.

"You . . . want to be loose . . . Sam . . . your body . . . your head." He stops scraping and looks at me, pointing the scraper to underline what he's saying. "You have to be ready for the unexpected. You may have the course memorized, but you don't know what's going to happen to you when you make your run. You might hit a bump you didn't see. You might have more speed than you thought you'd have. You have to be loose enough to react to whatever happens out there. You understand?" He cleans the scraper on his pants.

"Yeah." I rotate my neck. I have to be loose. I have to be ready.

"Good, because these babies are going to fly."

*——— **Fifty-two** ———*

I CLICK INTO my bindings, take a deep breath, and slip my hands through the safety straps of my poles. I pull the goggles off my neck and over my eyes, but because I'm not wearing a hat the strap is too loose and the goggles drop down over my nose.

"Damn." The idling turns to a trembling.

"Here." Mom pulls the strap toward her. I can't see

what she's doing. I only feel the goggles pulling against my neck. "How's that?"

I pull the goggles back over my eyes. They stay. "Thanks." I loosen the Velcro straps on my gloves, pull the gloves up over my wrists so that the fingers are snug, and then tighten the straps.

"There goes sixty-eight." Phil slaps his gloves together. They make a dull thudding sound.

"Yeah, good luck, sixty-eight," I say as I grip my poles and slide my skis back and forth. They feel as fast as wings.

"Good luck, Sam," Mom whispers in my ear and kisses me on the cheek.

"Thanks." As I glide over to the starting shack, I crank my boot buckles tight.

"Okay, old buddy." Phil puts his arm around my shoulder. "You know you can ski with any of these dudes. You showed us that two weeks ago. I'll tell you, if I had just finished racing and were standing at the bottom of this mountain right now and knew you were up here, I'd be plenty worried. This is your kind of course, Sam. This course was made for you."

"Yeah." My legs are trembling.

"I want you to explode out of the start. Make as straight a line as you can and don't hesitate in the steeps."

"Number seventy-two."

The racer in front of me disappears into the dark of the starting shack.

"Phil, I got to ask you something."

"Yeah."

"Duncan said there's a cranker."

"In the last ten gates where it dips?"

"Yeah." My voice quivers, my mouth and lips are dry. I can see myself in his goggles. The little kid with blond hair and freckles. What am I doing here? "Is it a tight red?"

"Yeah, and it's a cranker all right. Just be early on the blue before it and you'll be okay. This is your kind of course, Sam, fast and tight. It was made for kids like you who know how to turn. Just let your skis run and find your rhythm. Let the mountain sing to you."

"Yeah." My legs are a rough idle.

"Seventy-three, come in. You're next."

"That's us, Sam. Race you to the bottom."

"Yeah, right." I turn and glide through the door into the darkness of the starting house.

"You have thirty seconds to get yourself ready, number seventy-three."

"Thanks."

"Good luck, Sam," Phil yells.

Yeah. I roll my shoulders, bend my knees, and jump in the air. My skis slap down on the wet snow. I look down at the mountain. Out of the darkness, the course is as bright as a video screen. I curve my glove through the gates as if it were me. Attack the steeps, find the rhythm, let them fly. I take a deep breath.

"Ten seconds."

"Let them run, Sam."

I slide the tips of my skis underneath the starting wand. Carefully putting my poles over the wand, I jiggle them until they are firmly planted in the snow. I crouch down low and stare at the red gate just to the right, then at the blue gate back to the left. The red and blue panels are fluttering in the late-morning breeze. A few racers are watching on the side. Attack the steeps. Find my rhythm. Stay forward and let them fly.

"Racer, get yourself ready . . ."

The idling surges through my legs. I can feel it revving to a roar. This is my course. Good luck, Bo. Ride this one with me, Felix. I grip my poles extra tight.

"Five, four, three."

The roar gets so loud I can't hear the countdown anymore, so I go.

∗———— Fifty-three ————∗

I SPRING OUT of my crouch, throwing my boots and the tails of my skis up behind me. The tips of my skis dip. For a split second I hang suspended in the air. Then I swing forward and break through the wand. I explode out of the house into a shower of brightness. I soar toward the first red gate, crank the turn, soar back across to the blue, crank that turn, and soar back to the next red. The rhythm of the course has somehow gotten inside me like a song. I keep attacking, I keep picking up speed. And when I hit the steeps I'm flying.

I sing through the gates as if they're memory, carving through my turns. I plunge through the undergate, suck up the bump, and I'm into the flats. I tuck, my head just above my knees, my legs vibrating. Let the skis fly, Sam. Roll those ankles. This is your course. Remember the tight red, Sam. Remember it's coming. Over the crest where it drops. Be early on the blue. Be early on the blue.

I'm late.

Christ, how'd I get so late?

The red is way over to my right.

How am I going to get over there?

I rotate my hips out over the downhill ski. The ski compresses into a curve and carves radically right, catapulting me across the hill toward the red gate.

I land off balance on my uphill ski.

My arms are flailing like wings.

My downhill ski is up over my shoulder.

The red gate is rushing straight at me.

I'm going to straddle and die.

Blood roars out of my brain.

I pull at the ski and somehow it comes down as I soar through the red and turn back toward the blue.

Then, as if nothing out of the ordinary has happened, I'm back on both skis, running straight for the next gate. Feathers of sweat are sprouting all over me. Seven more gates. I go into a tuck, my head jiggling down by my knees, my hands in front of my face, my legs bonfires. I roll my ankles. My skis carve a straight line through the gates. I throw my poles across the finish line, spray to a stop, and collapse, my legs smoldering and my ears roaring. I try to catch my breath. I try not to puke. Slowly I get to my feet and glide through the opening in the orange plastic fencing, feeling as if I just died.

Fifty-four

THERE'S A CROWD of parents and racers hanging around the finish, talking and laughing. A voice announces a time over the loudspeaker, then pauses, and everyone falls silent. The parents are silent. The racers are silent. I try to catch my breath.

"One minute, please," the loudspeaker announces. "There's a correction on bib number seventy-three's time."

Everyone starts talking again. I glide through the crowd, and as I do parents and racers stop talking and back away from me as if I have chicken pox.

"Sam," voices call from the mountain. I turn around and Leah and Molly, Duncan, Josh, and Louie are racing down the last steeps straight at me. They spray to a stop, all five of them talking at once.

"What was your time?"

"I can't believe your ski was over your head."

"I almost fell."

"Your face is white."

"I'm going to throw up." I double over and wretch. Nothing comes out but saliva and tears. While I'm bent over I unbuckle my boots. Then I pull myself up on my poles and wipe my mouth and eyes. I feel dizzy.

"What was your time?"

"You were dead. I don't know how you stood up."

"What was your time?"

"I almost fell."

"You looked great."

Static from the loudspeaker. The announcer clears her throat.

"Shhh." Molly puts a finger to her mouth.

"Number seventy-three's time stands at 52.71 — "

"Fifty-two seventy-one?" Duncan yells.

"Our new thirteen-year-old leader with the fifth fastest time of the day is bib number seventy-three."

"Yes!" Molly shouts. "Yes!"

Leah and Molly slap me on the back and hug me.

"Unbelievable." Duncan pounds me on the back. "You're only three-tenths of a second behind me."

"Wait until Phil hears." Molly hugs Leah.

"Number seventy-four's time," the loudspeaker crackles, "is 58.95."

"Not even close." Leah shakes my shoulders. "Seventy-five is the last racer."

"Dumb luck," Louie says. "Dumb stupid luck. Any other kid would have fallen."

"Shut up, Louie," Leah says. "Will you, for once in your life, shut up?"

"He was lucky."

"Louie." Duncan looks at him, his head at an angle. "If Sam blew away Josh and Josh blew you away, you don't have to be a genius to figure out that Sam blew you away. Better get used to it."

"Used to what?"

"Used to Sam blowing you away."

"Number seventy-five, our last racer, is approaching the finish line. His time is fifty-nine seconds."

"Sam." Molly throws her arms around me. "Where's Phil? Where is my father?"

Duncan and Josh pound me on the back. Even Leah hugs me. "Congratulations."

"Here he comes. Dad." Molly shouts, jumping up and down and waving. Phil snowplows to a stop ten yards away from us.

"Dad." She runs up to him. "Guess what?"

"You won the lottery."

"Dad!"

"Okay, you didn't win the lottery. Leah won the lottery."

"Dad." She punches him hard on the arm.

"Ow. Okay, I give up. What happened?"

"Sam's in fifth place and he's the top thirteen-year-old."

His eyes whip across our faces and shine straight into my eyes.

"Is that right?" he asks me.

"Yeah." Leah punches me. "That's right."

"He's only three-tenths of a second behind me," Duncan adds.

"Is that right?"

"Of course it's right." Molly hits him again on the arm. "You think we'd make up something like this?"

"Well, I'll be." Phil snaps out of his skis. He comes over and wraps his arms around me. "I knew you had a good run in you, old buddy, but fifth place? Make my day. Fifth place? Not bad. Not bad at all."

"Yeah." I smile. Not bad for an alternate.

Fifty-five

WHEN I LOOK UP, Mom's walking down the side of the course.

I slide out of Phil's hug and start running toward her. My legs feel like celery.

"Mom," I yell at her when she's a hundred yards away.

"Sam." She waves at me. "How you do?"

"I'm in fifth place."

"What?"

"I'm in fifth place."

She starts running down the hill, sloshing toward me in her Sorel boots, Bo's green coat and purple pants flying off her shoulder like a cape.

"What did you say?" she asks, out of breath, when she gets to me.

"I'm in fifth place."

"That's what I thought you said." She wraps her arms around me and squeezes me so tight I can feel my heart beating.

"And I'm the first thirteen-year-old."

"Oh, Sam, I'm so happy for you."

Fifty-six

MY SECOND RUN is the heart of a dream. Phil calls it being in a groove. The heart of a dream repeats itself the way the heart repeats itself. Gate after gate. Everything about my second run feels as if it happened before. Slipping through the course, listening to Phil's strategies, imaging skiing through the gates, making the last-second adjustments, riding the chair, waiting at the top, worrying about the snow, about our skis, about the course, about our opponents. We wax with white paraffin. We cork and scrape. We cheer Molly and Leah. Then Phil has me warming up because I'm the first guy on our team to go. That's the only part of the afternoon that's never happened before. I feel that I'm cutting in line when I get ready to go. But then everything else feels the same. Phil's talking to me. The guys are yelling at me down by the second gate the way they always do after they've finished their runs. I listen to Phil telling me what I've got to do.

"It's your race, Sam. Don't let anyone take it away from you. Get out there quick, find your rhythm, crank those turns . . ."

While I listen, I watch the racers ahead of me attack the course. I study the red and blue gates, the GS panels fluttering in the afternoon breeze, the sky blue over the white snow. A hunger begins to whistle through me, leaving me empty except for the race. In the starting gate when I stare down at the course, I have this feeling I want to devour it. Then I'm on course, soaring down the mountain, cranking through the gates, gaining speed with each turn. I don't make many mistakes, and when I get to the bottom and the reps with company logos on their jackets come up and say, "Nice race, kid," I know my time is going to stand.

——— Fifty-seven ———

LEAH AND DUNCAN are going to get trophies, so Phil has us wait. It's part of what makes us a team, he tells my mother. We change our clothes, pack our duffels, load our skis in the van and truck, and then walk across the snow in our running shoes to one of the gray condos at the foot of the mountain. There's a gray deck overlooking the chair lift. It's built around an empty swimming pool. Most of the kids and parents have gone home. Just the ones who are getting trophies and their friends are waiting. We all sit together against the railing with the bench-seat. Half of us sit on the bench, the other half on the deck. The sun has set behind the mountain and a cold breeze washes down the slope and settles slowly around us.

It takes forever for the five officials to come out with their computer print-outs. Two of them are carrying a large cardboard box. They put the box next to a picnic table, then take golden trophies out of the box, and line them up so that they look like organ pipes. We all point and ask the same questions: Which one is Leah's? Which one is Duncan's?

One of the officials starts talking about what a great championship it's been. Even though I've never been here before, it's the kind of talk that I've heard a thousand times. I stop listening. The whole problem with trophies is they're like the lottery. There's not enough for everyone. Every racer on the mountain has a dream that ends with a trophy. But only a few get one.

They do the girls first. I watch Leah get her trophy and cheer her. She smiles, embarrassed, and then comes back to us carrying the trophy like an old bag. She scolds us for making too big a deal for third place, but she passes it around. It's heavier than I thought, a wooden base with a gold plaque and engraved lettering. The gold cup of the trophy is shaped like an old-fashioned cup, with gold handles big enough for doors. On top of the cup is a skier crouched in a turn.

Between the girls and the boys, one of the race officials says something about a special presentation. I hear him call a couple of names. A girl stands up. Leah and Molly push me.

"That's you," they say. "Get up."

"What?"

Duncan pushes me to my feet, and then everybody's hands push me toward the picnic table. The official has the girl stand on one side of him and me on the other.

"Since the IIIs are such a broad age group, from thirteen to fifteen, this year we have decided to acknowledge the first thirteen-year-old girl and boy."

I hear clapping and cheering like radio signals from

another planet. Then he calls off the girl's name and hands her a trophy. More cheering. Then he calls off my name. His voice and the cheering are like a movie that's out of focus. He hands me the trophy. It's heavier than I thought. I try to say thank you, but my voice and lips won't work together. My lips are dry and stuck shut. Thank you, I try to say, but what comes out of my mouth is a croaking sound. I feel that there's an extra gallon of blood pumping through my face. I sit back down. The kids pound me on the back and grab at the trophy. I let them take it. Then I just stare at the wood deck, wishing we were on our way home.

——— Fifty-eight ——–

WE DON'T SAY MUCH. Mom is driving and I'm sitting next to the shopping bag.

Winning a trophy is not what I thought it would be. I thought it would be like turning on a switch somewhere and everything would light up and be different. But it's not like that at all. Everything's the same. I mean, sure there's a celebration. When Mom and I got home there were congratulations signs over the doors and balloons everywhere. I don't know where Bo got so many balloons. There was even apple juice champagne, carrot cake, toasts, and Polaroid pictures of me with the trophy. Then me and Bo with the trophy. Then me and Mom. But nothing felt really different.

We pull into the parking lot. Our headlights flash over the trunks of trees and cars. Mom parks between a Ford and a Subaru.

"Want me to wait in the car?"

"If you want." I grab the shopping bag, run up the steps, and push through the double glass doors. I don't look at the painted lines on the gray linoleum floor. I jog down the corridor and up the flight of stairs, out into hall, and down to room 1028. The door's open.

"Hey." Felix smiles. He's lying in bed. "Congratulations."

"Phil's already been here?" I put the bag on the floor. "Yeah."

"That jerk." I sit down on the edge of the bed. His cast is still hanging from a wire. "How's the leg?"

"Still broken."

"Yeah," I say stupidly. I lift the bag off the floor and rest it on the end of the bed. "I brought you something."

"From the gift shop?"

"No." I hand him the bag.

"What's this?" He pulls the trophy out of the bag.

"It's yours."

"What do you mean it's mine?" He looks at the trophy, the golden skier crouched in his turn. "This isn't mine. I've been lying here for the last ten days with a broken leg. I haven't won anything. I haven't even been to a championship."

"I'm giving it to you."

"What a jerk." He looks at me. "You can't give this to me!"

"Yes, I can."

"No, you can't."

"It's mine, right?"

"So?"

"So I can do with it what I want. And I want you to have it."

"Yeah, well, I don't want it."

"If you don't want it, throw it away."

"I'm not throwing it away."

"Then *I'm* throwing it away." I grab one of the handles of the trophy.

"No." He holds on to the other handle. "Don't throw it away. Put it over there for me."

I put it on his bureau. "How's that?"

"That's good. Now I can look up at it when I want and it'll remind me."

"Yeah." I nod my head. "Remind you of what?"

"Remind me of . . . what a jerk you are," he says with his old smile.

———— Fifty-nine ————

THAT NIGHT, when the house is too warm, Bo and I go outside and sit in the snow in the back yard. Our backs are against each other. The cold feels good. It's so dark I can tell where the branches are only by the absence of stars. The white smoke coming out of our chimney catches the light from the street and lights up the dark angles of our roof.

Bo breaks the silence. "If you look at the stars you can almost feel the earth move."

"Yeah." When I lean against his back and look up at the stars I can feel the earth move. It feels good to be out here in the cold. It feels good to be out here with my brother. It feels good to know that the earth is moving and that the championships are already thousands of miles behind me.